Ready, Aim, Slocum!

Smollets watched as a figure was dumped unceremoniously onto the bed. He didn't think it was Slocum. He was big enough, all right, but Slocum didn't seem like a fellow foolish enough to fall off his horse and hurt himself.

Through the sights on the rifle, Smollets took careful aim at the big, wide-shouldered man walking away from the window and toward the door.

Smollets took a deep breath and held it in, steadying himself.

He fired . . .

JAKE LOGAN

SLOCUM
AND THE
FAMILY BUSINESS

JOVE BOOKS, NEW YORK

THE BERKLEY PUBLISHING GROUP
Published by the Penguin Group
Penguin Group (USA) Inc.
375 Hudson Street, New York, New York 10014, USA
Penguin Group (Canada), 90 Eglinton Avenue East, Suite 700, Toronto, Ontario M4P 2Y3, Canada
(a division of Pearson Penguin Canada Inc.)
Penguin Books Ltd., 80 Strand, London WC2R 0RL, England
Penguin Group Ireland, 25 St. Stephen's Green, Dublin 2, Ireland (a division of Penguin Books Ltd.)
Penguin Group (Australia), 250 Camberwell Road, Camberwell, Victoria 3124, Australia
(a division of Pearson Australia Group Pty. Ltd.)
Penguin Books India Pvt. Ltd., 11 Community Centre, Panchsheel Park, New Delhi—110 017, India
Penguin Group (NZ), 67 Apollo Drive, Rosedale, North Shore 0632, New Zealand
(a division of Pearson New Zealand Ltd.)
Penguin Books (South Africa) (Pty.) Ltd., 24 Sturdee Avenue, Rosebank, Johannesburg 2196,
South Africa

Penguin Books Ltd., Registered Offices: 80 Strand, London WC2R 0RL, England

This is a work of fiction. Names, characters, places, and incidents either are the product of the author's imagination or are used fictitiously, and any resemblance to actual persons, living or dead, business establishments, events, or locales is entirely coincidental.

SLOCUM AND THE FAMILY BUSINESS

A Jove Book / published by arrangement with the author

PRINTING HISTORY
Jove edition / July 2009

ISBN: 978-0-515-14650-9

JOVE®
Jove Books are published by The Berkley Publishing Group,
a division of Penguin Group (USA) Inc.
375 Hudson Street, New York, New York 10014.
JOVE® is a registered trademark of Penguin Group (USA) Inc.
The "J" design is a trademark of Penguin Group (USA) Inc.

PRINTED IN THE UNITED STATES OF AMERICA

10 9 8 7 6 5 4 3 2 1

1

By the time that Slocum rode into Sleepy Creek, it was nearly eight in the evening. Too late to have his Appy's loose shoe replaced, but not too late to find himself some dinner and some poker. Just so the evening wouldn't be a total loss, he told himself.

He found a hostler at the livery, got Speck squared away, and got directions to a café and a saloon. Not that he needed any. If Sleepy Creek were much smaller, he could have fit it in his back pocket. There was just the one main street, dotted here and there with shops and such, including both the café and the saloon. There was only one of each.

After a surprisingly good steak dinner with home fries and apple pie, he made his way down to the saloon, Harry's Bar by name. Like the town itself, there wasn't much to Harry's Bar. It was shaped like a shotgun's barrel, with a narrow, rough-hewn service bar and barely enough room for the barkeep to stand behind it. A few scattered tables ran down the other side. There were no pictures or paintings on the walls, just pegs from which lanterns hung. There were exactly two other customers in the place, and neither one looked like the cardplaying sort.

Slocum bellied up to the bar and ordered a whiskey with a beer chaser. He took his time drinking them. One of the other two customers down at the other end of the bar, a boy of perhaps sixteen, had caught his eye. Or Slocum had caught *his*. They stared at each other for close to five minutes, neither one blinking, until Slocum glanced down to put aside his whiskey and pick up his beer.

By the time he thought to look down toward the kid again, the boy was within three feet of him, and still staring.

"You Slocum?" the boy asked. "John Slocum?"

Slocum paused a moment. "Who's askin'?" he said at last, and took a drink of his beer. The last thing he needed—or wanted—tonight was another kid in his teens looking to make his reputation.

"Xander," the boy said. "Xander Crimson."

Slocum nodded, although the name didn't ring a bell. "Pleased to meet you, Xander. That short for Alexander?"

As the boy nodded, Slocum looked him over. He was a little over six feet tall, Slocum guessed, with sandy red hair and green eyes, and he had a coating of trail dust on his clothes. He'd been traveling, too.

The boy stood there for a moment, as if trying to muster up the courage to ask Slocum something, and then he suddenly blurted, "Did you ever know a woman named Cissy Carter?"

Slocum furrowed his brow. The name was vaguely familiar, but it took him a moment to place it. "Didn't she used to work over in El Paso, at the Crystal Slipper?" That had been a dive, too, as he recalled, but the women who worked there were at the opposite end of the spectrum from the premises. And Cissy, as he recalled, had been a real hell of a beauty. Red hair, green eyes, just like—

"You're my daddy," Xander said with a quick nod, as if it were the most matter-of-fact thing in the world.

Slocum, as shocked as he was, took a closer look. The boy surely didn't have his coloring—except for the green eyes—but his build was as lanky and gangly as Slocum's had been at that age. There was just the first hint of muscle in his shoulders, arms, and legs, too, as had been the case with Slocum. Red hair and green eyes ran in Slocum's family, although both his ma and his pa had been of a darker complexion.

"How old did you say you were?" he asked.

Xander furrowed his brow. "I didn't. But I'm sixteen. I was sixteen last September."

Slocum did some quick math in his head. Sixteen—no, seventeen—years ago in January, he had been in El Paso, and he'd been with Cissy Carter—as many times as possible. It was the last time he'd seen her. But apparently, not the last time she'd found something to remind her of him. As much as he hated to admit it . . .

He looked Xander square in the eyes. "Yes. I could be your father."

The kid surprised him by laughing out loud, then hugging Slocum so tightly that he thought the boy might bust his ribs. Slocum heard him mumble, "My pa, my pa . . ." And when Xander was finished hugging him, he found that he had to wipe away tears of happiness and surprise.

So did the boy.

"And so I was about three when Fred Crimson married Ma and adopted me," Xander was saying. "Ma made sure I knew you were my pa, though. I mean, my real one. She even swiped a wanted poster from the sheriff's office one time because it had your picture on it." He stopped to dig into his pocket, and produced a carefully folded paper, which he offered to Slocum. They were seated at a table for two by now, opposite the bar. And they were the only customers in the place.

"Fred Crimson died four winters back," the boy offered.

Slocum said, "Sorry."

"Wasn't that big a loss," Xander said, his mouth twitching to one side, and didn't offer anything further. Slocum wondered if the boy had been mistreated, but right now didn't seem like the time to ask.

Slocum unfolded the paper. It was him, all right, although it wasn't the best likeness, and it was for a crime—a robbery—for which he'd been cleared better than ten years ago.

Grinning, he handed the paper back to Xander. "Hope you don't think I go 'round bustin' the law every six seconds."

"No, sir," Xander replied. "She said it was more like every five or so." And then he broke out into a grin. "Naw, she said you were a . . . what'd she call it? Oh, yeah—a 'perpetual victim of circumstance.' That's it. I reckon she loved you till the day she died."

Slocum felt that last sentence like a hard punch in the gut. "S-she's dead? Cissy's dead? What happened?"

Xander carefully refolded the paper and tucked it back inside his pocket. "Cancer," he said, his voice thick. "Doc did everything he could, but . . ." His eyes, starting to brim with tears, dropped to study the table's scarred top.

"So you're on your own then?" Slocum asked.

Xander nodded. "Except . . . except for you. If you'll have me, that is."

Slocum didn't know what to say. Except for the hair color, it was like looking into the face of a portrait of himself at that age. But still . . .

"Aw, hell," he finally grumbled. "I wouldn't know what to do with you. Ain't got no home 'cept whatever scrap of desert I decide to lie down on of an evening. I'm no good for you, Xander. You oughta be back East, goin' to school. You're a sharp kid. You could make somethin' of yourself."

"I could make something of myself with you, too," the boy said. "I'm a good shot, and I've got my own horse. Ma told me all about you. You've done pretty fine by yourself these last few years. I read all the dime novels about you, every single one, and I been trackin' you since you left Bitter Root, Nevada."

Slocum shot up a brow. "That's nearly a year back!"

The boy nodded. "Yes, sir."

A loud voice from behind the bar called, "You fellers gonna keep nursin' them same beers, or can I close up now?"

Slocum pushed his chair back with a scrape. The boy followed suit, and tagged after him to the batwing doors. "Go ahead and close," Slocum called to the bartender. "There a hotel, or do strangers have to sleep with their horses?"

The barkeep hiked a thumb up the street, indicating that they should go north. "Miss Carolyn's boardin'house. Closest thing we got to a hotel."

Slocum said his thanks, then pushed through the doors, followed by the boy. Stride for stride, they walked up the street, the reluctant father and the eager son.

While they were introducing themselves to Miss Carolyn— who turned out to be a spry sixty-six-year-old with at least three cats—and getting settled in at the boardinghouse, the barkeep was blowing out the lanterns back at the saloon and thinking about getting home to his pretty wife and his nice, soft bed. He had just come to the last lantern, the saloon keys jangling in his free hand, when the batwing doors swung in.

Muttering, "Well, shit!" under his breath, he turned toward the sound.

A lone cowpoke stood there in the dim light of the doorway. "You're closin'," the cowpoke said.

The barkeep took advantage of the moment, and replied, "Yessir, had some slow-drinkin' fellers in here what wouldn't leave." He blew out the last lantern, but when the cowpoke didn't budge, he added, "Want to get on home and see the wife. We're expectin'." Then: "The baby's due any day now."

The cowboy in the doorway still didn't move an inch, didn't twitch a muscle.

"Is there somethin' I can help you with?" the barkeep asked, a tad nervously. Now that the last light was out, the shadowy figure in the doorway seemed ominous, looming. "S-somethin' I can get for you?"

At last, the figure spoke. "The boys that took too long with their drinkin'. Was one of 'em 'bout six foot, dark hair, green eyes? Have a scar on his neck?" He ran a finger across the back of his neck, just under his hairline, to indicate that the scar was horizontal.

Now, this feller was seeming more and more like trouble with each passing second. And if there was one thing the citizens of Sleepy Creek were allergic to, it was trouble.

The barkeep slowly shook his head. "Sorry," he said, holding his voice steadier than he would have believed possible. "Don't recall nobody with a scar. And the last customer I served was a redheaded kid. 'Fraid I don't take much notice of eyes."

Slowly, the man in the doorway dropped one shoulder. "He's in town somewhere. Pretty sure one'a those Appaloosas down at the livery is his."

"Mister, I spent the whole afternoon and evening back behind that bar with one trip to the outhouse out back. If somebody rode in on a polka-dot Indian elephant in one'a them sedan chairs, I'd be the last man in town to hear about it."

The stranger grunted, then turned and disappeared. The barkeep heard his retreating footsteps going south, down toward the livery, and only then did he pause to wonder how in the bloody hell a man got a scar across the back of his neck. A bullet or a blade, he figured. A bullwhip maybe, but unlikely. A hanging rope was at the wrong angle. And if a feller got a scar like that, no matter how, why hadn't he died from the wound?

Shrugging, the barkeep at last headed for the front doors, stepped through, and locked the heavy outer doors. Not that there was much chance anybody'd break in.

The denizens of Sleepy Creek were much as the town's name implied: law-abiding, but more out of laziness than anything else. The barkeep liked it that way.

Quietly, he stepped around the side of the saloon and up the outside stairs to his living quarters, head shaking, thinking, *Damn strangers. Nothing but trouble.*

2

The next morning, Slocum took advantage of the breakfast spread put out by Miss Carolyn. She turned out to be a roaring good cook, and provided a long table filled with fried chicken, fried eggs, bacon, toast and jam, cold roast venison, fried potatoes, oatmeal, and various pickled vegetables.

Slocum filled up on chicken and venison, plus an enormous side of potatoes: enough that he figured he wouldn't have to eat for a couple of weeks.

But by the time he was half finished with his plate, Xander still hadn't shown up. He hadn't answered the knock on his door either. Slocum had mixed feelings about this—if the boy was truly gone, it saved Slocum saying his good-byes, and then again, maybe the kid hadn't been his son after all. But if he was still in town, where the hell was he?

His questions were answered momentarily, when the front door banged and in walked Xander, all smiles and good-mornings.

Slocum waited until the boy had filled his plate and taken a seat at the table before he said, "Been out?"

Xander, busy buttering his toast, looked up long enough to say, "Yeah, been down to the livery."

Slocum's brow furrowed slightly. "The livery?"

"Yes, sir. They're gonna fix your horse's shoe the first thing, once the farrier gets in. 'Bout eight." Xander took a big bite of buttery toast and commenced chewing.

"Thank you," Slocum said slowly. To be honest, this "maybe having a kid" thing had thrown him into an uproar. He felt like his brain was a green salad, being tossed around by a restaurant waiter. He looked down the table again at the redheaded boy. Yes, there were plenty of similarities, but plenty of Cissy's physical characteristics were in there, too. What if Cissy had just preferred men of his type? Big men with Irish backgrounds, men who'd be moving on soon.

Anything was possible, no matter how much—or how little—he'd like to believe the boy's story.

It was obvious that Xander intended to ride out with him, though. His trip to the livery and orders for the farrier proved that. And Slocum wasn't at all certain how he felt about it. Not that a traveling companion was a bad idea, not at all. It was just that he didn't know if this was the right one for him, particularly with Goose Martin on his trail.

Old Goose had been dogging him for the last couple of weeks, seeing as he'd laid the fault for the deaths of his brother, Bill, and nephew, Badger, at Slocum's feet. Slocum hadn't even been in Lonesome at the time, although he rode through a couple of days later, but somehow the rumor that he'd back-shot the Martins, father and son, had taken hold.

Any port in a storm, Slocum figured. He just didn't like

being Goose's port of call. And he didn't appreciate having to watch his back as close as he had since word reached him that Goose was hunting him. Goose had a reputation, none of it good. He'd nearly got Slocum only ten days ago, when he was riding outside the town of Redport. Goose's slug had just slithered across the flesh on the back of his neck—another fraction of an inch, the doc said, and it would have severed his spine. It was healing now, but Goose had added another scar to his collection.

It stank. And son or not, he surely didn't want the kid mixed up in that situation, let alone taking a bullet meant for him.

Something caught his attention, and he looked up from his venison. It was Xander, saying, "Dad?"

For a second, Slocum was stumped as to who the kid was addressing. But then he caught himself, and said, "Yeah?"

"What do you think?"

Slocum was stumped. "About what?"

Xander and Miss Carolyn chuckled: Xander, out loud. Miss Carolyn tittered softly behind her hand. They were her only customers for breakfast. Hell, by the looks of the town, they might have been her first customers in a couple–three years. Or more. At any rate, she seemed thrilled to have them there.

Xander waved his hand. "Oh, nothing, Pa."

"Nothing important," said Miss Carolyn. "Enjoy your breakfast, Mr. Reed."

"Mr . . . ?"

Xander cut him off. "Pa, there was a stranger sleeping in the livery when I was down there."

"A stranger?" He was about to ask how the hell Xander would know a stranger from a longtime resident, but stopped when he realized if the boy had been here for an hour or two of daylight, he'd have probably met everybody.

"Yup. He woke up while I was tellin' the hostler about your horse's shoe."

Slocum nodded. "Thanks. Nice of you."

"I thought he was awful nosy. He was askin' our names and what you looked like and where we were goin' and stuff."

Slocum stiffened. But then the boy added, "I told him you were Jake Reed and I was your boy, Xander, and we were headed down to Phoenix. We are goin' to Phoenix, right?"

For Miss Carolyn's benefit, Slocum nodded yes.

He said, "This nosy feller. Don't s'pose he gave you his name, did he?"

"Only part of it, but I figured that was made up, on account of he said it was Goose. We ain't never met nobody named Goose, have we, Pa?"

Slocum relaxed. The boy had inherited the Slocum trait of telling a story with a straight face, all right.

"I do believe that if we had," he replied, "I'd have remembered somebody named Goose."

Miss Carolyn stood up and began clearing the food off the table and sideboard. When she disappeared into the kitchen, Xander whispered, "I did right, didn't I?"

Slocum nodded. "You did perfect. When did they say the farrier'd be in?"

"Eight or thereabouts."

Slocum checked his watch. It was eight ten. He snapped the case closed and slipped it into his pocket, saying to Xander, "Want you to go back at about nine. If Goose is still there, I want you to saddle both horses and lead mine up here behind yours. I reckon Goose'll still be there. He asks any more questions, tell him I've got the croup or somethin'. I can ride, but I'm too sick to walk to the livery. And he asks about Speck—the horse I'm ridin'—you tell him that we bought him off a horse trader over in Sylar City sometime last week, and that I'm real happy about the trade."

The boy nodded. "Right."

Slocum waited inside the boardinghouse, peering down the street through a lace-curtained window in the parlor. And about a half hour after he'd left, Xander came riding up the street on his own red Appy, and leading Speck behind him. With his eyes still on the livery, Slocum waited until the boy had tied both horses at the rail and entered the building before he looked away.

"We ready?" the boy asked.

Slocum almost told him right then and there, the way he had been planning, but the look on Xander's face was too eager and excited for Slocum to do anything but go along.

"Ready," he said, and strode toward the boy and the open doorway, wondering just how far he'd have to go to shake Goose off his tail.

When the kid had come down to get the horses, Goose had questioned him about the other Appy. He'd been wondering about the horse ever since he'd first seen him—it had been described to him, and this one sure fit the bill: a dark liver chestnut with a star and a snip on his face, three white socks, and a snow white blanket over his rump that carried only three medium-sized oval splotches of liver chestnut. He'd been certain that this was the same gelding that had been described to him not once, but at least three times.

Well, it had been described once as a stud—and as a

pinto— but that feller had been about two weeks out of New York City and drunk to boot, so Goose hadn't put much faith in him.

But when the kid stood there in front of him and swore to God that his pa had picked that horse up from a trader up to Sylar City about a week ago, Goose had to think about it. And when the kid added that his pa was sickly and that they were headed north, it gave Goose further pause.

He waited until the kid took off, leading the liver chestnut behind his sorrel, and then he hid around the corner of the livery. He watched while the kid stopped and tied the horses in front of the boardinghouse. When the boy came out again, he was propping the elbow of a man older than himself—and perhaps an inch or two taller—a man who stumbled twice and coughed once before he got himself up into the saddle. The kid wasn't more than three inches from him the whole time, like he was afraid his pa would take a fall if he wasn't there to catch him.

So Goose let them ride out, even though the older man's hair color was dark. But lots of men had dark-colored hair. And he wasn't able to see his face, since the man had kept his head tucked down, away from view, the whole time— either because he was in pain, or because he was attempting to hide his face.

But it was still bothering him come noon. And bothering him even more by two o'clock that afternoon. By three, he couldn't stand still. He saddled up his horse, paid the stable man, and set out for the north at a soft gallop.

While Goose was starting north, Slocum and Xander had already ridden in that same direction to a rocky place where Slocum knew the ground wouldn't carry a track. There, they turned to the west, then to the south, partially circumnavigating the little town, and were a quarter of the way to Phoenix. And Slocum still hadn't figured out a way to tell Xander he wasn't welcome to ride along.

The kid seemed so . . . happy, that was it, just plain thrilled. And so chatty, and so eager to see what'd be around the next bend.

Slocum couldn't find it in his heart to tell him that he wasn't wanted. And to tell the truth, Slocum did want him along. As long as it was safe, that is. He'd be damned if it would be said that Slocum had found a son and gotten him killed, all in the same day, or even in the same week.

3

Slocum and Xander camped about fifteen miles north of Phoenix. Slocum figured they'd ride into town early. He didn't know if Xander had any plans, but he had his mind set on visiting Miss Pearl's whorehouse. Maybe for a day or more. They hadn't seen one sign of old Goose, and Slocum was hoping that they'd lost him for good. Of course, getting up close and personal with Goose was the only way to end this for good and for all, but it wasn't something he wanted to happen while his son was along.

His son. He'd found himself thinking of Xander more and more in that context as the day had worn on, even though there was still a part of him that didn't want to believe. He'd find himself musing over sending the kid back East to college—although where the money was going to come from was anybody's guess—and then catch himself, and wonder why on God's green earth he was thinking about putting out that much money for somebody who was practically a stranger to him, somebody who'd been lied to by his whore of a mother.

And then he'd catch himself again.

That's how it had been all day. Back and forth, and back and forth again.

"Pa?"

The word startled him, but he quickly regained his composure and looked across the fire at the boy. "What?"

"More coffee, please?" Xander said, extending his mug. He couldn't seem to wipe that grin off his face.

Slocum lifted the pot and poured the kid a cup. Maybe something would happen tomorrow to change the boy's expression.

He was going to make the kid buy his own sugar, that was for sure. He'd never, not in his whole adult life, met such a fiend for sweets as this kid.

He stopped himself again. His cousin Dave, who he'd met just once when he was five or six, had been even crazier for sugar than Xander was. He remembered his Aunt Ella saying she had to bake something every day to keep Dave, who must've been about Xander's age, happy. And that must've been some feat, seeing as how they were on their way to Texas in a great big Conestoga wagon. Well, maybe it hadn't been all that big. After all, that was a long time back. But he remembered that the top of his head didn't quite clear the center hub of the wheels. And he'd been big for his age, too.

So, maybe it came down the genetic pike to Xander quite naturally.

No.

Yes, but . . .

Aw, hell.

*   *   *

Xander sat in silence as he watched Slocum toss his dinner scraps into the dying cookfire, clean his plate with desert sand, then stretch out near the fire, his head on his saddle.

As Slocum pulled his hat down over his eyes, Xander mouthed a soundless, "Night, Pa."

He couldn't believe his luck in finding Slocum. After nearly a year of riding from town to town, territory to territory, here he was, finally right across the fire from him! And he had turned out to be exactly as Xander had imagined him—tough but tender, a rough customer who knew when to run and when to fight. He was courtly to old ladies—their night and breakfast at Miss Carolyn's had proved that—and he could drink with the best of them. Well, Xander couldn't really be certain about that part, but he'd seen the way that Slocum had handled a couple whiskeys and a couple of beers back in town.

He had faith in everything Slocum had ever done, and faith in everything he might do in the future. To him, Slocum was like one of those fabled knights in shining armor, the kind they used to have over in England. Except he doubted that they had Appaloosas way back then.

He thought that over for a few minutes, the dying fire crackling and popping as he stared into it. No, he finally decided, no Appies in England. Or even over in Ireland, for that matter.

He finished his coffee. He would have liked it sweeter, but he didn't feel right using up Slocum's last little bit of sweet. If he'd known what Slocum was up to this morning, he would have gone to the mercantile and got himself a pound or so. But that was water under the bridge, and tomorrow, Slocum had said, they'd ride into Phoenix. Phoenix! Even the name was magical!

Grinning his perpetual grin, he cleaned out his mug,

found a flat place to lie down, and did so, to dream happy dreams through the night.

Come morning, Slocum and Xander hit the trail early, and were nearly to Phoenix by nine thirty. The boy was visibly excited, although Slocum could tell he was trying to hold himself back from yammering. He had told Xander not to get too excited—that Phoenix might be one of the biggest cities in Arizona, but compared to Kansas City or San Francisco or Denver, it didn't mean shit to a tree. But Xander, being a kid, wasn't having it. Looking at his smile, you'd think they were riding into El Dorado.

He'd still seen no trace of Goose and he took this as a damn good sign, although Goose still had to be out there somewhere, lurking. Slocum figured that Goose would follow the new logger's road only so far before he'd figure out he'd been duped. Then, it'd be only a question of direction, and Slocum was hoping it wasn't south. From Phoenix, he was planning to head down that way, almost to Tucson, to Hiram Walker's ranch. Hiram had wired him a few weeks back. Something about his cattle disappearing.

Well, if Hiram had rustlers, Slocum figured he'd make short work of them—in exchange for some handsome recompense from Hiram, of course. Hiram paid well, and Slocum figured to make enough on this deal to send him burrowing his way through every box of fine Havana cigars—and every last bottle of the best French champagne—in the whole of the Arizona Territory.

But what was he going to do with the boy?

By two in the afternoon, Slocum didn't have time to think about Xander anymore. He was too busy with the captivating Miss Juanita, who Miss Pearl had said was "my best."

And after three go-rounds, Slocum had little reason to doubt her. Juanita was as Mexican as her name would suggest, but she spoke perfect English, with no trace of an accent. Her figure was hourglass-shaped: full-busted, with round, brown, perfect orbs of breasts; tiny-waisted; and voluptuously hipped. She needed none of the body padding—or boning—that fashion encouraged most women to take advantage of.

And then there was her face. It was as delicate as a child's, unfurrowed and untroubled, free from the lines and creases that inevitably came with the worries of adulthood and making a living. She seemed not to have a care in the world.

Her eyes were as deeply brown as her hair was black, her lips bow-shaped and the color of roses. They were the same color, in fact, as her nipples and the tenderest flesh deep between her legs.

She was an accomplished lover. Slocum figured she must have been with a lot of out-of-town men to know the things she did. And he taught her a few new tricks, too.

They were just resting up from their last go-round, which had been real whizbanger, with the both of them ending up on the floor, her straddling him sideways, and the rug wrapped halfway round his head. Which was actually good, because it dampened the decibel level when he came and shouted out her name in a moment that was a curious mixture of shock, pleasure, and unadulterated joy.

They'd made it back up on the bed eventually, although he didn't remember exactly how, and now she lay curled up in the crook of his arm, intermittently drowsing and humming softly. *Well, it isn't exactly a hum,* he told himself. *More like a . . . purr.* He smiled at the thought, and softly said, "My little kitten . . ."

She roused slightly at the sound, blinking and muttering, "What?"

He cupped the back of her head, tangled in curls, in the palm of his hand. "Nothin', baby. Hush now. Go back to sleep," he murmured. Her eyes closed again, and he felt the fight against sleep go out of her.

He felt his eyes slowly close as well, and it wasn't long before he, too, fell soundly asleep.

Xander was in hog heaven.

Slocum had bought and paid for a girl for him, too: a cute little speck of a thing, no older than he was, who went by the name of Taffy and who told him that she'd just started there, having just come west from Ohio.

She was a beaut, all right, with straight and shiny flaxen hair, and blue eyes the color of cornflowers. Beneath fair, blond eyebrows that you could barely see, the lashes were lush around those blue orbs, and the nose was thin and fine. Her lips were broad and she smiled a lot, which Xander found favorable, seeing as how he figured her job couldn't be all that pleasant most of the time. He figured that she must have to take men upstairs from time to time that weren't to her liking. She seemed to like him, though, seemed to like him quite a bit, as a matter of fact. She'd told him so anyhow, and she'd . . . well, she'd showed him, too.

A grin spread across his face, a grin so broad that it couldn't have been shut down by the biggest slice of chocolate cake in the world. His ma had always made chocolate cake for his birthday, till she got sick.

His smile faded. He missed his ma something fierce. He knew he probably shouldn't—kids missed their folks like this, not practically grown-up men—but he couldn't help it.

She'd seen that he got his schooling, that he knew his manners and how to act like a gent, that he knew all about the birds and the bees and how babies got made, and she'd also kept his "father," Fred Crimson, from beating him bloody each time the whim took hold of him.

Xander had loved her like crazy. But not the way he loved his little Taffy. He tickled her beneath her chin, and in her sleep, she smiled. His grin popped back into place, too. Boy, this was every bit as good as his ma had told him it would be once he got around to it.

Taffy dozed beside him. He'd have to thank his pa, too, thank him in a big way. After all, he'd given the girl to Xander for the whole of today and tonight, too, and it wasn't even dark yet! He wondered just what the proper thanks was for nearly twenty-four hours of monkey business with a pretty blond girl. Right at the moment, he couldn't think of anything nearly nice enough.

Slocum twisted in his chair. He and Juanita had come downstairs for a bite of supper, and Miss Pearl had just said something to him.

"Beg pardon?" he said while he slid Juanita's playfully grasping hand away from his crotch.

"I said there was a man here lookin' for you," Miss Pearl said again. "Don't remember the whole thing, but his first name was Goose. Be a long time before a body'd forget *that*."

Slocum grinned and said, "And?"

"Told him what you asked me to," she replied. "He went away, but I don't know how far."

"Thanks, Pearl," Slocum said, and nodded. Goose had found the trail again, damn it. "He shows up again, you tell him the same."

She smiled. "Naturally. Oh, and I was just out in the barn. Grained your horses. They'll be fine until morning."

Again, Slocum said, "Thanks, Pearl." She had a shed out back of the whorehouse—jokingly called "the barn"—where those in the know, or on the run, could put up their horses for as long as they needed, so long as they paid for their upkeep. Slocum, followed by a curious Xander, had ridden there directly upon entering Phoenix.

To Pearl, he said, "I ain't heard a peep outta Xander. You know how he's gettin' along?"

Pearl grinned infectiously, her salt-and-pepper head bobbing. "Oh, I think they're gettin' along just fine, Slocum. Don't you worry. Taffy's one'a my best."

4

The next morning, Slocum woke Xander about nine. They grabbed a quick breakfast downstairs, and had left Phoenix behind by a quarter to ten. Xander, who'd just had time for a quick run up to the mercantile, was newly stocked with peppermints, horehounds, a pocketful of suckers, and enough sugar for his coffee to last him to Tucson. And then some.

Slocum left town feeling relaxed, thanks to Juanita, and with a pocketful of fresh smokes, courtesy of the Phoenix tobacco shop. He hardly ever had a chance to avail himself of ready-mades, and so he took the chance when he had it. Now that they'd left the town behind and were on the long, desolate ride south toward Tucson—and still no sign of Goose—he tipped the pack from his pocket and opened it.

Beside him, Xander took the sucker from his mouth long enough to say, "Thanks, Pa. I mean, for Miss Pearl's place and all. It was . . . it was . . ."

Slocum flicked a lucifer and held it to the tip of his

smoke. He blew out the match and dropped it on the trail while the kid was still trying to form a sentence. "It's all right, Xander," he said before he took a long drag. "No problem. Hope you enjoyed yourself." Smoke jetted from his nostrils in twin streams.

"Oh, yes, sir!" the boy exclaimed. "Miss Taffy was just . . . , just . . . just lovely! She was *grand*!"

Slocum laughed. He didn't mean to, but it had to come out. He tried to remember if he'd been so, well, *buoyant* after his first visit to a whorehouse.

When he turned back, Xander was staring at him rather oddly. Slocum said, "Sorry, boy. Wasn't laughing at you. Just tryin' to remember how I felt the first time I visited a whorehouse."

"And?"

"Don't rightly recall," Slocum answered with a shrug, then smiled. "Hope I felt as good as you do, though."

This time it was Xander's turn to laugh, and Slocum chuckled along with him. An ease was beginning to develop between the two, but Slocum still wondered: Was it just because they were experiencing the same conditions, or was it something more, something natural?

After spending one night on the open desert, Slocum and Xander arrived at Hiram Walker's ranch late the following afternoon.

Hiram, a portly fellow of medium height with an affable countenance centered by a huge handlebar mustache, met them with a big grin on his face, although he seemed a little confused about the boy. "You taken on a trainee there, Slocum?" he asked while he pumped Slocum's arm up and down in a seemingly never-ending handshake.

"No, Hiram," Slocum replied, once he got free of

Hiram's tight grip. "Believe Xander here"—it felt uncommonly strange to say it out loud, but he did—"is my son."

Hiram blinked rapidly, muttered, "Say what?" then turned toward the boy. He grabbed Xander's hand now, and began to pump it enthusiastically, saying, "By God! Slocum's boy! By God!" over and over.

Once Hiram and Xander disentangled themselves, Hiram asked them both up to the ranch house, where, he said, his cook ought to have dinner just about ready.

"Still got Katie doin' the vittles?" Slocum asked as they slowly walked up the path. Katie had cooked for Hiram the last time he was visiting, and she hadn't liked Slocum one bit. The feeling was mutual.

But Hiram said, "Nope. She found herself some button salesman out of New Jersey to run off with. Now I got me Samantha. She's a better cook, too."

Slocum smiled. He was hoping she was more friendly than Katie. He didn't think it was possible for Samantha to be any more hateful than Katie had been toward him, so that gave him some hope. It had to get better, didn't it?

A hand met them, received Hiram's orders to grain the horses and put them up for the night, then lead both Appies down toward the horse barn. "Should'a known it," Hiram said with a chuckle. "Should'a known it by the ass-end of those horses a'yours. Like father, like son!" He led them up the steps and opened the door. "Well, come on in, you two."

He led them into the parlor, and sat them in overstuffed leather chairs. Hiram had gone a long time before marrying, and his taste in furnishings showed it. There was nothing even faintly feminine about the room.

"Got your telegram yesterday, Slocum," Hiram began as he stepped toward the small gentleman's bar in the corner.

"Sorry to say the thievin's still goin' on strong. Lost another five head last night, accordin' to the boys. I know that five head don't sound like much, but when it's been keeping up for as long as it has, it turns into a bigger number. A hundred and sixty-seven head to date."

He handed Slocum a bourbon and branch, and gave the same to Xander. "Just sip on that now," Slocum muttered. And then in a louder voice, he asked Hiram, "If you been losin' cattle all along, why'd you wait so long to get hold of me?"

Hiram shrugged. "It was so slow! Thought it was coyotes at first, or maybe a puma. Hell, even a jaguar. We get one or two this far north every now and then, y'know. But we never found any track. Just cattle track, and then nothin'."

"Nothin' at all?" Xander asked. He was downing that bourbon quite a bit faster than Slocum had recommended, and Slocum slid him a dirty look.

Which Hiram missed entirely. "No sir, son," he replied. "It was like them cattle just up and disappeared mid-stride." He paused to take a sip of his own drink. "Like they got swept up into Heaven or somethin'. But what's God want with a handful of range-bred, half-Hereford cattle?"

Before anyone could think of an answer, a young blond man, dressed in a servant's fancy livery, appeared in the doorway. "Sorry to interrupt, sir," he said to Hiram, "but dinner is served."

Goose was camped for the night on Slocum and Xander's trail. As he waited for his stew to cook—he'd been lucky and brought down a couple of skinny jackrabbits—he pondered his situation.

He was fairly certain that the boy had lied to him, had

given him a false name. And he knew that he been lied to about the direction they were headed. North, his ass!

He'd gone on after their trail ended, gone on a good ways. But it had never picked up again, and first he'd scouted to the east, then to the west, where he'd finally found the track again. Their trail had headed straight south.

Still, he couldn't help but not hold the boy liable for his actions. Slocum, that murdering coward, had doubtless put him up to it.

Goose had little time for murdering cowards, let alone a man who'd let a boy hold him back from a certain scrape. Additionally, the boy, Xander, looked almost exactly like the nephew that Goose had been told Slocum had shot in the back. He was about the same age, too, maybe a year or so older. Like his nephew, Slocum's traveling companion reminded Goose of himself when he was in his mid-teens, back before his hair started to get shot through with gray.

He gave the stew another halfhearted stir and sat back again. Yessir, there was something about that kid. He didn't know what it was, but there sure was something.

Dinner was a very formal affair, with a linen tablecloth and napkins, more food than Slocum had seen in a week, a young footman or housemaid behind each chair to refill the wineglasses while they were still half full, to snatch away empty plates and replace them with the next course, and to constantly ask if everything was to their satisfaction, plus a young boy seated on a stool in the corner, pulling on the rope that turned the ceiling fan overhead. As Slocum and Xander ate, Hiram told them more about the thefts, then drifted into the everyday.

At last, the main course arrived—an inch-thick steak, prime cut, with all the fixings—and Slocum was unashamedly plowing into his when the constant buzz of Hiram's ongoing oration ceased.

Slocum looked up to find both Hiram and Xander staring at him expectantly.

"What?" he asked.

"Mr. Walker just asked what your plan was, Pa," Xander blurted out.

Slocum grinned. "Sorry, Hiram. This beef a'yours is so good it took all my concentration." He wiped his mouth on his dinner napkin. "Don't rightly know that I've got enough information to form a plan as yet. But tomorrow mornin', Xander and I'd like to see the place those last head disappeared from. Scout the territory, like that."

From over his shoulder, a footman asked, "More peas, sir?"

Slocum nodded. No wonder Hiram had put on weight since the last time Slocum had seen him. "Been meanin' to ask, Hiram. Where's Betsy? She gone off to Boston again?"

Hiram smiled. "Yes, she has, both she and her sister. I expect them back toward the middle'a next month." He looked toward Xander and added, "They always go back East durin' the hottest part of the summer. Hell, if I didn't have these thefts happenin' right and left, I was plannin' on goin' with 'em this year!"

Xander nodded, and Slocum said, "Maybe next year, Hiram."

Hiram nodded, although somewhat dismally. "Hope you're right, Slocum. I plan to go with 'em every year, but there's always somethin'. If some thieves ain't stealin' my cattle, a well gets poisoned or a passel of hands up and leave, or . . . Aw, hell. It's always somethin'."

Slocum chuckled softly. "Maybe it just ain't meant for you to go to Boston, Hiram. You'd be outta your element.

All that figurin' out which fork to use and such." He'd noticed that, at least during Betsy's absence, Hiram had held the tableware down to a knife, fork, and spoon. Thank God.

Dismally, Hiram nodded. "You're probably right, Slocum. Never understood why my Betsy married me in the first place."

"Why, Mr. Walker?" Xander piped up. "You're a good man, and you got yourself a real nice ranch."

"The boy's right, Hiram," Slocum went on. "Hell, she probably counts herself lucky, having landed an even-tempered cowman from Arizona!"

Hiram mused on this for a silent moment, then suddenly said, "What's wrong with you boys? Dig in before it gets cold!" And he dived into his steak. Slocum and Xander had no trouble following suit.

5

The next morning, after a breakfast of waffles with butter and raspberry syrup, eggs cooked to order, thick, smoked bacon, and good, strong coffee, Slocum and Xander saddled up and left the ranch house behind, accompanied by Apollo Gomez, Hiram's foreman and all-around headman. Although Apollo's father had been Mexican—and a first-class hand himself—his mother had been a Negress freed by the war, and Apollo had eyes and skin as ebony as she'd had. He was as tall as Slocum and nearly as robust, but walked with a slight limp.

"Yeah, got kicked by a bronc in just the wrong place," he explained to Slocum and the boy on the ride out. He'd been very chatty all the way out, having told them about his parentage and background, and how he'd come to work for Hiram.

"Will it go away?" the boy asked. "The limp, I mean."

"Seein' as how I got her about ten years back, I don't reckon she'll get no better than she is," Apollo replied matter-of-factly. "Guess I'll always have a little hitch in my gitalong." He pointed ahead to a break in the cliffs. "Down that way's where they disappeared. Them and the prints both."

Slocum squinted toward the break. It didn't look like much of an opening to him, and it sure didn't look like it'd go back through the rock, but then, he was pretty far away from it.

"It's around thirty feet across," Apollo said, as if he were reading Slocum's mind.

Slocum snorted softly before he said, "Thanks. I was wonderin'."

Slocum had been right about one thing—the crack in the wall was indeed pretty far away. It took them over an hour to get up to it, riding at a jog, and once they got there, Slocum was pleased to see that Apollo had been correct—it was roughly thirty feet across at the opening, and traveled back, slicing south, into the mesa for as far as he could see.

"Apollo," he said as the Appy pranced a bit beneath him, eager to move again, "what's the closest thing up that way?" He pointed straight behind him.

Apollo shrugged his shoulders. "Phoenix, I reckon."

"No," said Slocum. "I mean *any*thing."

"So do I, Slocum," Apollo said. "And that'd still be Phoenix. Might be a couple'a jackrabbits, a coyote or two, and some bugs along the way, but—"

A grin quirking up his lips, Slocum held one hand up toward Apollo. "I get the picture," he said. "How about to the south?" He pointed down the chasm in the rock.

"Well, this dang thing cuts a crookedy path clean through to the other side of the mesa," Apollo said. "On past that, there's Tucson. And the Santa Ritas, of course.

Closer, but off to the west a bit, there's Casa Grande. You know, that big old pueblo?"

Slocum nodded.

"And Picacho Peak," Apollo went on. "Y'know, I never did understand that. Why anybody'd name that rock twice."

Slocum laughed, and when he saw that Xander looked confused, he said to the boy, "Picacho Peak. Picacho means Peak in Spanish. So, basically, it's Peak Peak." He grinned. "Or Picacho Picacho."

Xander's quizzical look turned into a smile. "Oh, I get it. I heard tell of the Rio River once. Same difference, huh?"

Slocum nodded. "Same difference." He turned back to Apollo. "Let's see where those tracks vanish."

"Not far from here," Apollo said as he nudged his mount into a slow jog and led them south, into the mouth of the chasm.

About a half hour later, after traveling over terrain walled by red-streaked granite and floored by loose, gravelly sand and increasingly less and less vegetation, they came to the end of the trail. The tracks of five steers were simply there one second and gone the next.

Slocum looked around the canyon—which at this point had grown to about fifty feet wide—for anything that the rustlers might have cut a wide branch from, for it was obviously a brush drag. He spotted a lone and very scrawny paloverde over toward the east wall. "Ride on over there and see if there's a recent cut where a branch ought to be," he said to Xander.

The boy lit out like his horse's tail was on fire.

"Brush drag?" said Apollo. When Slocum nodded in the affirmative, Apollo said, "Figures. Me and one of the other boys followed about halfway down the canyon here, and didn't see a blessed sign. It's a long way to haul brush, though, and still keep it in one piece."

"Not if you keep on gettin' new brush," Slocum replied as Xander came galloping up. "Find anything?" he asked the boy.

Xander nodded. "Yessir. 'Bout halfway up, there's been a thick branch cut off. Looks like it was done with a pocket knife, what with all the sawin'. Was a big'un, too. You can see the gap from here." He pointed, and Slocum noticed the wide, airy V in the already thin upper formation of the paloverde.

"Good job," Slocum said, and the boy grinned happily. Slocum turned toward Apollo. "I guess we're gonna go on down south. You comin' with us, or does Hiram have your afternoon planned out already?"

"'Fraid it's the last one," Apollo said. "But I'll tell him where you are. When you reckon to be back?"

Slocum shook his head. "Don't know," he said. "When I'm done, I guess. Xander?"

The kid's head flicked up like an eager retriever's. "Yessir?" If he'd had floppy ears, they would have been cocked.

"You're comin' with me."

"Yessir!"

An hour after they said good-bye to Apollo, they were still wandering south through the canyon, which grew sometimes quite a bit wider, and sometimes thinned down so much that they had to ride single file, their knees and elbows scraping the walls.

Slocum kept an eye out for any sign of track—a part of a horse's shoe, a half of a cattle track—or anything that might have been left behind. But it was Xander who found the first sign.

They were enduring one of those narrow places when, from ahead, Xander called out, "Hair on the wall!"

Slocum moved his horse up behind Xander's, and there on the wall was a sure and certain sign of a Hereford cross— deep red brown coat underlined with white hair. There wasn't much of it: just a patch about a palm's breadth wide where the passage wall jutted inward a couple of inches and the rock was especially coarse and rough. But it was there.

"Guess they didn't think to drag that brush up high enough, did they, Pa?" the boy said. His face fairly glowed with achievement and the excitement of the chase. He was keen for tracking, all right.

"Right, you are," Slocum said, and took advantage of the halt to pull out a ready-made and a match. He flicked the sulfur tip to life on the rock wall pushing at him. "At least we know we're goin' the right way." *And that the cattle are somewhere up ahead,* he should have added, but instead, took a long drag on his smoke.

They moved on, eyes alert, senses keen.

After another hour or so, with no further sign to be seen, Slocum noticed something curious about the wall to his right and hollered to Xander, across the canyon, to hold up a second. Slocum jogged over to the wall.

The brush piled up and pushed into a crevice hadn't been pushed there by any wind, but placed there by human hands. When he climbed down off Speck and took an even closer look, he could see that some of it had been roped together, too.

A glance over his shoulder showed that the kid was still plodding toward him across the canyon, but this couldn't wait. He moved Speck over a couple of feet, and began to tear at the brittle brush that clogged the opening.

It came out fast, especially once he got his hands on a loop of the rope holding the plug together. By the time Xander stopped his horse and got off, Slocum was through to the other side, staring at perhaps twenty-five head of cattle munching hay or nibbling at the sparse desert vegetation. Someone had set up a stock tank for them as well, and hauled water in from someplace.

"Well, I'll be jiggered!" Xander said. He was at Slocum's left side, eyes bugging at the sight of all those cattle. "You ever seen the like?"

Slocum nodded. "Not exactly, but close enough." He was remembering that cattle scheme up in Montana a few years back. Not exactly the same game, but enough like it to ring a few bells in his head. But Ring Darby and three of his men had been hanged by the Montana cattlemen, and the two other boys Slocum had caught were still cooling their heels in prison. But there was no rule that said the same idea couldn't occur to two different men in two different places.

"What?" The kid had said something, and Slocum stared at him.

"I said, what are we gonna do now?"

Slocum had been planning on visiting Pamela's House of Pleasure down in Tucson, but it looked like that was out of the question for a while. He said, "We're gonna bring our horses in here, and our butts in here, too, then block the opening back up."

"And then what?"

"And then we wait."

Xander's brow wrinkled. "For what?"

"To see who comes to pick up those cows.'"

It was nearing darkness. Xander and Slocum had made a small camp at the northernmost curve of the box canyon, and they had just finished piling wood for a cookfire when something across the way caught Xander's eye.

"Wait!" he hissed at Slocum, who was just making ready to light the fire's kindling. "Over there!" he said, pointing upward.

Across the canyon, there was a harnessed horse standing at the rim, and a moment later, a man carrying a bag of something walked up next to it. As Xander and Slocum watched, the man bent low and shifted his burden to the ground, then opened it and poured out water. The water fell with a gush and landed in the stock tank. Several cows ran toward it and dipped their heads to drink.

The man disappeared again, and once again came back bearing a heavy bag, repeating the process. In fact, he brought a total of four bags of water to the rim and poured them over the rim and down into the stock tank. Xander couldn't figure how it would possibly fill the tank, but it would surely knock the dust up a few inches.

And then the man vanished again and came back toting a hay bale. This, too, he pitched down into the canyon, and followed it with three others, one at a time. Xander was tired just watching him.

When the man disappeared the next time, Xander looked over to see Slocum at attention: eyes narrowed, his hat pulled low, sitting on his heels behind a stray tumbleweed. Once he saw Slocum's expression, Xander knew he'd done right. He was proud of himself, but not so proud that he allowed himself to look away from the cliff any longer. He turned his gaze again toward the opposite rim.

The man started carrying up water again. In fact, he carried so much up and dumped it down into the stock tank, that Xander figured that stock tank must've been extra deep or something. Hell, maybe there was another tank butted up right behind it!

About the time it got too dark to see much across the way, the shadowy shape of the horse moved, turning away and pulling the dim outline of a wagon behind it. And then he couldn't see any shadow or outline at all, nothing but black emptiness.

After a few minutes had passed, he whispered, "Is he gone for real this time?"

In response, Slocum scratched a lucifer into light and lit a ready-made. After he took a long drag, he said, "I believe he is, Xander. And we know somethin' else, too."

Xander leaned toward him. "What's that?"

"We know they ain't plannin' on pickin' up them cattle tomorrow."

"We do?"

Slocum nodded curtly, his eyes still on the opposite rim. "They put down enough feed and water to last this bunch over twenty-four hours. Thirty-six, more like. I reckon they won't be comin' for 'em till the day after tomorrow."

6

The next morning, Slocum and Xander took down the canyon's sagebrush barrier. Xander waited outside to turn back any cows who tried to veer south, while Slocum rounded up the herd and pushed them through the opening. After the last animal was through, Slocum followed her out into the canyon, and called to Xander, "That's the last of 'em. Is everybody headin' north?"

Xander nodded, smiling. He was clearly enjoying this little "adventure" and was looking forward to the next step.

Slocum said, "All right, let's herd 'em back to Hiram's place. If we're lucky, we can make it by lunch."

Xander looked disappointed. "But I thought we were gonna go south today!"

"No point in it," Slocum replied. "They won't be back until tomorrow at the soonest." Then he added, "Don't worry. We'll come back."

While Xander's frown turned into a smile, they started pushing the cattle north, back where they'd come from.

Slocum had a plan, all right, but it likely wasn't one the boy expected.

Two hours later, while Slocum and Xander were still pushing cattle north through the canyon, Hiram walked out on his front porch to find that a stranger was riding toward the house. The lone rider was close enough that Hiram could make out his build and coloring, and at first glance wondered if Slocum had sent for his brother.

But no, that couldn't be right. Slocum didn't have any brother, at least not one that Hiram had ever heard him speak of. And really, this stranger looked more like Xander than Slocum. Same coloring anyway. Hiram held up his arm and waved a greeting.

The rider waved back with an empty hand, to show he meant no harm, and rode on up to the ranch house. He spoke first.

"Howdy," he said, starting to dismount, then caught himself.

"Howdy yourself!" Hiram replied, and added, "Get on down and have a sip. Ain't often I get company."

The stranger dismounted then, and tied his horse at the rail. When he got to the porch, he stuck out his hand and Hiram took it, saying, "Hiram Walker, at your service, sir."

"Goose Martin, Mr. Walker. Pleased to meet you."

"Call me Hiram, and I'm pleased to be met," Hiram replied as he ushered Martin into the house, then inside the parlor. He'd been wishing for an excuse to open his little bar for the last hour. "What can I get for you, sir?"

Goose smiled. "You can stop callin' me sir, for one thing. I'm just Goose." He sat down in a chair. "And I'd like a bourbon and branch, if'n you got any."

"Indeed, I do," Hiram replied, and fixed one for Goose,

then one for himself, then sat down across from his visitor. He took the first sip of his drink. "And what brings you out our way, Goose?" His ranch, being far off the beaten path, didn't attract many visitors.

Goose drank down half his drink in one gulp. "Lookin' for a man. Big feller, 'bout my height and build. Dark hair, with green eyes, I'm told. He's got a fresh scar back here." Once again, he drew a line across the back of his neck.

Without thinking, Hiram said, "I don't know about the scar, but sounds like you're talkin' about Slocum."

Goose sat up straight. "He around, or did he ride on through?"

"Oh, he's out on my range right now, takin' care of my rustler problem," Hiram said. "He's quite a man, that Slocum. Always manages to get the right angle on any situation."

Without feeling, Goose replied, "Yeah, I've heard that."

"You a friend of his?"

Goose stood up and headed for the small bar. "You mind if I help myself?"

"No, go right ahead." Hiram was beginning to have an odd feeling about this visitor. "Did you say you were a friend of Slocum's?"

Goose, fresh drink in hand, came back and sat down again. "Nope, never met him. Met his son a couple–three times, though."

Hiram relaxed a little. Any friend of Slocum's son was a friend of his, and he said so.

Goose nodded his acknowledgment, then asked, "So you're having rustler trouble down this way? Lost many head?"

Hiram poured out his woes, and Goose proved to be a good listener. He listened for almost an hour, in fact, before he turned the conversation back to Slocum. "Where is he right now?" he asked.

"Oh, hard tellin', hard tellin'," Hiram said. "Your best bet's just to wait for him here. Go on and put your horse up out in the stable, then come on back up to the house. Seems to me it's gettin' about time for lunch!"

Out with the cattle, Slocum had called a halt to the proceedings to stop and take a leak against a cluster of barrel cactus. Xander sat in the saddle about fifteen yards to the north, keeping an eye on one steer that had tried more than once to outfox them and run back to the canyon.

Xander intended that the steer wouldn't succeed. And Xander had gotten his way three times, twice in the canyon and once out here on the open flat. But Slocum hadn't told him that the steer had made two other attempts, both of which had been foiled early on by Slocum and Speck.

Slocum liked Speck a great deal. The Appy had cow sense and lots of it, and could turn on a bottle stopper to boot. He didn't know if the Appy came by his savvy naturally, but he sure as hell had it.

Slocum hoped that this was one horse that wouldn't get shot out from under him. He'd like to keep Speck around for a while. Actually, he'd like to keep him around until he retired to his ranch—a recurring fantasy—and let him live out his days grazing on clover.

Now, he'd have to change that fantasy to include Xander. He wasn't sure how exactly, but it'd have to change.

He buttoned himself back into his jeans, and hollered, "Speck!" The gelding came more readily than an old hound dog. Slocum swung up into the saddle and resumed pushing the cattle.

Xander said, "How come Hiram's got so many cows mixed in with his steers? Or why are the thieves stealing so many heifers?"

"That last might be the better question," Slocum said. "Reckon it's a smarter man's game to steal breeding stock, 'specially if he's got the time to take advantage of 'em."

Xander screwed up his face. "Huh?"

"If a feller's got him a spread close enough by, got access to a breedin' bull, and a brand that's an easy switch, he's not only stealin' cows, he's stealin' generations of cattle with each heifer he takes."

"Okay," said Xander, nodding. "I get you now."

"Good," Slocum replied, with only a tiny afterthought that any son of his should have figured that simple truth out by himself. "I believe we're only about an hour out from Hiram's house now. What you say we cut that down some?"

Xander smiled at this and sucked in enough air to let out a most jubilant yelp and yahoo, and they stampeded the cattle into a dead run that would eventually end—although at a bit slower pace—in Hiram's holding pen.

Later, while the milling cattle settled in, Xander secured the gate while Slocum checked to see that they had water. Which they didn't. He hollered up to Apollo, who knew the system, and who opened the sluice gate to the trough, saying that he'd see that the stock got fed.

Xander and Slocum led their horses into the barn, fed them and put them up, then trudged their way up to the house, hoping to find lunch waiting.

What they found was lunch, all right, but someone that Slocum didn't at all expect was eating with them.

Goose Martin.

* * *

Goose was in the middle of a sentence when Xander and Slocum walked in, and he stopped cold, in the middle of a word.

Hiram looked up and said, "What was that, Goose?" before he saw Slocum and the boy. Then he clambered happily to his feet, asking rapid-fire questions about his missing beeves.

But Slocum and Goose had locked eyes, and were busy appraising one another. To Goose, Slocum suddenly looked a good bit bigger than he'd been led to believe. To Slocum, Goose was exactly what he'd expected.

Slocum spoke first. "You lookin' for me?"

"That I am," Goose replied, his face implying no misgivings. "Seems like I found you."

"Sit down, boys, sit down!" cried Hiram, tickled to be present at the "reunion."

Xander took a few steps to the side and hissed, "Quiet, Mr. Walker!"

"It's Hiram, son," the rancher boomed jovially before he caught the boy's meaning and sat quickly in his chair with a muffled: "Oh. My goodness."

Still looking at Slocum, Goose didn't change his expression, but he said, "Goodness ain't got nothin' to do with it, does it, Slocum?"

Slocum had barely begun to open his mouth when, much to his surprise, Xander jumped in between them. "My pa didn't do it! He wasn't even in town!"

"Hold on there, Xander," Slocum said, and gripped the kid's shoulder, moving him out of the way. "You want to ride with me, there are a few rules. First off, I like to hear a man say his name before we start talkin'."

"Goose Martin," the man said, still staring. "Brother to Bill and uncle to Badger."

"John Slocum," Slocum said with a nod. "'Fraid I didn't know your brother or your nephew. Sorry, though. I heard about 'em when I rode through town."

"More like when you shot 'em." Goose's body posture had changed dramatically.

Slocum shook his head. "Mr. Martin, I'm a pretty good hand with a gun, but not even I can shoot from two days away. Truth is, I rode into Lonesome on the seventeenth of last month, spent the night in the hotel—believe it was called The Stockman's—and left the mornin' of the eighteenth. You can check with the hotel or the livery."

"Why should I believe anything that comes outta your mouth? Hell, your boy there has been lyin' to me ever since I first seen him!"

"Now, don't take it out on him," Slocum said. "He's just been doin' as he's told. What say you wire The Stockman's up in Lonesome—or the livery there. What's the name of it? Red's, that's it. Red's Livery. Hell, wire 'em both! See if I ain't tellin' you the truth."

It was the best Slocum had, and he slumped into a dining chair. Xander tentatively sat beside him.

There was a long silence.

At last, Hiram couldn't stand it any longer. His voice breaking the gloom, he said, "Well, my goodness, let's get some vittles into you boys! I wanna see you eat your fill, and I wanna know what you found out about my rustlers!"

Slocum, smiling slightly, shook his head. "Don't have your rustlers yet, Hiram."

"But we brought back twenty-five head of those stolen beeves," Xander cut in.

"Wonderful, wonderful!" cried Hiram. "A magnificent start! Don't you think so, Goose?"

Goose held his silence and didn't speak. Whatever he was going to do, he'd have to do it later.

7

In his wheelchair, Cord Whipple traveled laps around the wraparound porch at his ranch. Something was wrong. Something was definitely off-kilter. Yesterday, for the umpteenth time, he'd had a wagonload of hay go missing in the middle of the day. It wasn't altogether suspicious. After all, the hired men had free rein to enter the hay barn and hayloft and take what they wished, for whatever purpose suited them. But why take hay—and baled hay at that—in the middle of summer, and furthermore, why haul it off to who knows where?

He stopped the chair so that he was overlooking the east range, and set the brake. Since his accident, he'd thought he'd run the ranch the same as always. Well, not from horseback or foot. But at least, he thought, the ranch was doing well and he was making money. Not a lot, what with the market having fallen off a tad, but enough to keep him going and pay the hands.

Compared to his neighbors, he was doing all right, he supposed.

But what on earth was going on with these little hay thefts? At first, he'd ignored them. Then, he'd puzzled over them, his curiosity having been piqued. But he was past that now. The thefts had turned into a full-fledged mystery. Nothing that would interest Mr. Edgar Allan Poe, of course, but one took what one could get. And this one, Cord Whipple had surely gotten, whether, as his pater used to say, he wanted it or not.

He was almost ready to have the surrey brought 'round, and drive the ten or eleven miles up to his closest neighbor's ranch—that would be Hiram Walker's outfit, the Walking W—and see if he was having similar problems. And if so, just what the hell he was doing about them.

Back at the Walker spread, Apollo Gomez and another hand finally walked over to the holding pen, into which Xander and Slocum had herded the twenty-five head they'd thought had been stolen. Apollo hiked his elbows along the top rail, then pushed his hat back. "Heifers," he said. "Mostly heifers. Again. I'll be damned."

The hand next to him, Bodie Crane, said, "Don't know why you'd be surprised. Heifers is mostly what they been swipin' since it started."

"Just that I can't figure what they're doin' with 'em," Apollo said in reply. "Have to be a spread fair close to us, one that's already got crossbred cows. Else-wise, they'd stick out like sore thumbs. Hell, some of those crossbreeds are seven-eighths pure by this late date. Trouble is, the neighbors what raise stock have got crossbreeds 'bout as far along as ours."

"Can't think of no neighbors what'd steal stock," Bodie

mused. He slipped his hat off and rubbed at his yellow hair, then clapped the hat to his head once again. "No, sir. Not one."

"That's the problem. We got us a crime with no suspects."

Bodie nodded. "Sure looks that way, don't it?"

Apollo nodded. "It surely does."

After lunch, an angry Goose wrote out telegrams of inquiry to both Red's Livery and The Stockman's Inn up in Lonesome. He also wrote one to the sheriff's office. He was taking no chances.

Hiram called a kid up from the barn and Goose gave him money for the telegrams, and the kid rode out to go into Tucson. "And you wait for a reply," Goose growled at him just before he left. The kid had looked scared to death of him.

Good.

And now, here he was—still in enemy country, so to speak—down by Hiram's barn, looking at a pen full of yearling cattle. Hiram was as jovial as he'd been all morning.

"In a box canyon off the Cut, you say, Slocum!" he was expounding. "I didn't even know there *was* a box canyon off the Cut! I'll be damned! I'll just be damned!"

Slocum looked up from the ready-made he'd just lit. "Easy there, Hiram. You still got about what? A hundred and twenty-some head out there? And we ain't exactly got any rustlers hogtied either."

Hiram just couldn't stop effusing. "Twenty-five head! In a box canyon!"

"I should'a had that extra piece of pie," Slocum grumbled.

Goose was thinking much the same thing. Except that he was thinking that he should have shot Slocum right in the center of his forehead, and then had another piece of pie. Hell, Slocum was probably thieving those cows himself, and had probably brought back these just to . . . just to . . . well, just to *something*.

He allowed himself a slight grin that almost registered on his lips. Slocum would look good with a bullet hole square in the middle of his forehead. Real classy, like they said back in Kansas City.

Xander, who'd been watching the nonverbal interplay between the two men for some time—ever since they'd walked into the dining room and found Goose sitting there, in fact—finally found his tongue. He sidled up to Slocum and said in his ear, "I think we ought to go on back tonight, Pa. In case those rustlers come back, you know?"

Slocum turned toward him and opened his mouth just as Hiram cut him off. "You know, fellas, I think you both need to set those guns in another room and get this thing between you settled. Without anybody gettin' killed, I mean."

Hiram must have been reading Xander's mind, and Xander heaved an audible sigh of relief. Slocum cocked a brow, whatever that meant, and said, "That's a good idea, Hiram. I'm all for talk, especially if there's another piece of pie connected with it."

Talk? Jesus! thought Xander. *I been ridin' with you for days, and I figure two grunts in a row is a lotta talk for you to spew out!*

But Goose nodded yes, and Hiram led them all back up to the house, with a reluctant Xander bringing up the rear. Good gravy, he'd just found his pa. He didn't want to lose him tonight!

He kept his eyes on Goose's gun. Goose was keeping his eyes on Slocum's.

Goose pounded his fist on the dining room table again, shouting, "You done it! I know you did!"

Slocum, sitting nonplussed, eating his third piece of pie, put down his fork and said conversationally, "Goose, I never met you or your brother or his son. If there was a Bible here, I'd swear on it if I thought it'd make you see reason. Let's try again. Why on God's green earth would I have a reason to shoot and kill two men—sorry, a man and a boy—who I never met, who never done me wrong, and who I couldn't identify if somebody was to pay me?"

"Maybe it was by accident!" Goose retorted. "Mayhap you wasn't gunnin' for them at all. Mayhap you figured it was two other fellers!" He nodded firmly, as if he'd finally figured the reason for good and all. "Maybe whoever hired you to do the killin' found out you screwed up, and mayhap he's already sent somebody after you, to kill you in your sleep." He turned to Xander. "Pass me that whiskey, kid."

Xander scooted the bottle down the table, then sat back again. He didn't look as if he was fond of the way things were going.

Slocum wasn't either. If the truth be told, he'd be just as happy to pull a gun and shoot Goose straight through the heart just to shut him up. But he didn't. He had to set a good example for the kid. Plus which, he didn't figure Hiram would be any too fond of bloodstains all over his dining room.

Quietly, he said, "No, Goose, that one falls apart, too. If somebody'd hired me, you can bet your ass I'd make certain sure of the target, and certain sure he needed killin'. 'Sides, I don't make package deals."

"Maybe you shot Bill, then Badger turned and saw you!"

Slocum sighed. The afternoon was long gone, and he was tired. And hungry for more than pie. "You're clutchin' at straws and feathers, Goose. Hell, if you want me to, I'll ride back to Lonesome and help you find who done it. But—and this is the last damn time I'm gonna say it—it wasn't me."

Hiram suddenly shoved back his chair and got to his feet, startling Xander and Goose. "Supper time!" he called, and immediately the doors to the kitchen and the butler's pantry flew open. Servants who had been as quiet as mice all afternoon quickly poured in, carrying fresh table linens and silverware and stacks of plates and replacements for the flowers that had centered the table at noon.

"Arms up, son," Hiram said, and the moment Xander complied, the tablecloth was changed, plates and silverware appeared in front of him, a freshly ringed napkin was beside his place setting, and someone set a glass of water on his other side.

"Holy cats!" the boy whispered, and Slocum chuckled. He knew just how the boy felt, having almost shot a manservant the first time Hiram had called for a meal while they were talking at the table.

That had been three years ago, the last time Hiram had had his tit caught in the wringer and paid Slocum to help him get it out. Hiram had been newly married then, and not two days after Slocum's arrival his new wife, Betsy, and her sister, Cordelia, had left to go back East, visit friends, and spend a great deal of Hiram's money. That last part, Slocum wouldn't have stood still for, but it seemed to tickle Hiram. Let it be, Slocum had decided, and he wrapped up Hiram's difficulty within the week.

On that occasion, the thieves had been part of Hiram's own crew, and Hiram had been a great deal more careful about who he hired and why ever since.

This time wasn't going to be so easy, Slocum thought as a pretty pair of kitchen maids placed a platter bearing a roasted goose on the table before him and another one, filled with baked apples and pears, before Xander. Bowls of mashed potatoes, stuffing, peas and carrots, and *refritos* came out, along with freshly churned butter, half a block of cheddar cheese, salsa, applesauce, and tortilla chips, still warm.

One thing about Hiram: He didn't skimp on the vittles. And it looked like this time, they were serving all the courses at once. This appeared to be a dandy arrangement, according to the expressions of the men seated around the table.

As a manservant traveled around the table, pouring out steaming coffee, a grinning Hiram said, "Well, don't stand on ceremony, boys. Dig in!"

Far out on Hiram's range, Milo Herrick had loaded up his wagon, and was very nearly at the edge of the cliff where the cattle were. This was his job, and he did it every night just before sunset. Water and hay, water and hay, the same thing every night.

He pulled up the rig at the very edge, climbed down, and walked to the back of the wagon, hauling down the closest object, which was a bale of hay. He struggled a bit hauling it down—the bales weighed a hundred pounds each—but he finally got the upper hand and hauled it to the rim. He tossed it down to the side of the water tank, and when he did, he noticed that most of the hay he'd left last night was still there.

He scowled and looked out farther, across the little box canyon. No cattle. No cattle? It wasn't possible!

He scrambled up to the wagon seat and pulled out the pair of binoculars secreted beneath the bench. He looked hard and far, but still no cattle.

And then he saw that the brush they'd used to plug the opening was gone. Just plain gone!

He set the binoculars beside him on the seat and lowered his head into his lap. How could this have happened? Especially after all the cattle they'd stolen so successfully, and over such a long period of time! A handful here, a handful there . . . They'd been doing it for years, and nobody had noticed, nobody! At least, not until now. Not until they began looting Hiram Walker's stock.

It wasn't fair, it just wasn't! He didn't think they were truly hurting anybody. Smollets agreed with him, and Smollets ought to know. It was his operation, wasn't it? Of course, Milo believed everything that Harvey Smollets said, according to Milo's brother, Turk.

Forget Turk, Milo thought, almost ashamed to be having private thoughts at a time like this. This was an incomparable calamity, and he was the one who was going to have to tell Harvey Smollets about it!

As he reined the buggy horse away from the rim and slowly began to plod back toward headquarters, he was nearly in tears at the news he was bound to deliver. What would they do if the sheriff came 'round?

And more important, what would Smollets do to *him*?

8

Hiram had some awfully nice mattresses in his guest rooms, but not one of his guests slept very well that night. Slocum, who usually could sleep like a log when he willed it, found himself tossing and turning and trying to figure out which of Hiram's neighbors was stealing his cattle. He'd learned that Cord Whipple, whose ranch was about ten miles south—and whose last name made him immediately suspect—ran a brand that also was a W, although it was a lassoed W, presumably lassoed by a cord. They called it the Cord W.

Other ranches in the area included the S-Bar-Q and the Rolling A. None of which did Slocum any good at all.

And then there was the mess with Goose. Slocum knew that Goose wasn't going to believe him until those telegrams came to prove that he hadn't been in town when the murders happened. But Goose seemed to be a stubborn son of a bitch, and maybe even that wouldn't convince him.

Goose lay awake most of the night, too, trying to figure out the best way to kill Slocum with nobody seeing. Out on the range would be a good idea, but then, the kid would be around. He liked the kid too much to shoot his pa in front of his eyes, although he couldn't really explain why. By rights, he should have killed the boy, too, to make up for his lost nephew, Badger. An eye for an eye and a tooth for a tooth, that was what the Good Book said. And that was exactly what Goose planned to give Slocum.

Xander, too, was restless. He was trying to figure out how to prove that Slocum hadn't been responsible for the deaths of Goose's brother and nephew, but he'd be hung out to dry if he could figure a way.

And to tell the truth, he wasn't certain that Slocum *hadn't* been the one who'd killed them. He'd read all the books about Slocum. And his mother, who'd been telling him about his true father for as long as he knew what she was saying, had also told him that she'd loved Slocum with all her heart, but that he was ruthless and deadly with that cross-draw rig of his.

Hiram, on the other hand, slept like a baby, certain that all his problems were about to vanish.

He was wrong.

Harvey Smollets wasn't home.

When Milo reluctantly took himself up to the house, the fireplace was cold and there was no coffee to welcome him. Harvey had gone visiting, and so Milo went on back down to the bunkhouse, where, finding that place deserted, too, he climbed straight into his bed and went to sleep.

Harvey Smollets, a tall, thin man of British descent—and accent—poured himself a third cup of coffee and sat back. His host, fellow Britisher and rancher Cord Whipple, took a puff on his pipe.

"What do you think, Smollets?" Whipple was asking.

Smollets tipped a head heavy with feigned indecision. "It beats me, as these Americans say," he replied. "If all you're missing is a small amount of hay . . ." He shrugged.

"Damn it, Smollets, it's the principle of the thing, don't you see?" Whipple said angrily. "I mean, who would possibly steal hay, for God's sake!"

Smollets sipped at his coffee. "I don't know, Cord," he said at last. "Are you certain your men aren't using it up themselves on your stock?"

Whipple shook his head. "Don't you think I haven't checked on that?"

"Of course you have, old man," said Smollets with feigned sympathy. An apologetic "Sorry" followed it. He tipped back his cup and finished his coffee, then set it down on its saucer. He sat forward. "Well, I'll certainly keep my eye peeled for your hay, Cord. Sorry to hear you're having trouble. But I'd best stumble along now." He stood up and bowed slightly.

Whipple, who couldn't rise, said, "I couldn't talk you into another slice of torte?"

Smollets laughed. "There you go again, trying to put meat on my bones! I assure you, Cord, I'm fine, just fine."

Whipple shook his head. "All right, have it your way. But thank you for dropping by. I was in sore need of someone to talk to."

"And thank you for welcoming me. I was in sore need of supper!" Smollets replied with a laugh. He walked to the front door and put his hand on the latch. "Well, be seeing you, Cord. I'll be keeping an eye out for your stolen hay, as I said."

"Thank you, old man," said Whipple, his fingers tapping

on the wheels of his chair. "I'd appreciate anything you could do to help me get to the bottom of this mystery."

"Well, then, good night." Smollets stepped through the door, saying, "You take care of yourself now."

"I shall," replied Whipple. "Ride safe."

Smollets closed the door between them and untied his horse from the rail. Mounting up, he made a mental note to tell his boys to stop stealing Whipple's hay. Cord Whipple was one of the few people around he could call a friend. He didn't want to lose that advantage over such a niggling little thing as a few hay bales.

By the light of a moon nearing full, he began his long ride home.

Slocum rose before the dawn, having gotten a total of about a half hour's sleep, and wandered downstairs, hoping the kitchen help rose as early as he had.

When he found the kitchen, he was pleasantly surprised to find a pretty young woman standing on tiptoes, trying to pull a big bag of sugar down off the top shelf.

"Let me help you," he said as he came up behind her. His voice startled her so that she fell, stumbling to one side, while the sugar bag tipped down and fell into Slocum's arms with a soft thud. The girl caught herself on the countertop and pulled the sugar bag from Slocum's arms before he had a chance to fall into her.

"Thanks!" they said at the same time, and then they both laughed.

Now it was his turn to take the heavy bag back from her, and he carried it to the table. He said, "Sorry, didn't mean to startle you," as he set it down, then pulled out a chair.

She smiled at him and said, "You're Mr. Slocum, aren't you?"

Sitting, he grinned back. "Yes ma'am, that's me. And you're . . ." He stopped to remember. "You're Samantha? Right?"

"Right you are," she chirped. She had wavy, light brown hair, tied back with a pale blue ribbon that matched her apron—and her eyes. Those were fringed with long, thick lashes a shade darker than her hair. She appeared to be in her early twenties, Slocum thought, and best of all, she was single. There was no ring on her finger.

"Are you down early for breakfast, Mr. Slocum?" she asked as she lit the stove.

"Somethin' like that," he replied, "although I gotta admit I wanted to take a sneak look in the kitchen, too, to see who was cookin' them great meals for us."

"Guilty as charged then," she said, filling a teakettle from the kitchen pump. "And you may call me Sam, Mr. Slocum."

He grinned and nodded. "It's just Slocum, Sam."

She smiled agreeably, and Slocum felt his pants getting tight. When her back was turned for a moment, he wriggled, trying to get comfortable. It didn't help very much.

He willed himself smaller, and at last it worked. Some. He was still uncomfortable. He asked, "What is on the menu this morning, Sam?" hoping that small talk would take care of what he couldn't will away.

Half an hour later, it had worked. He'd found out what they were having for breakfast—also lunch, although he wouldn't be here to take advantage of it—and that all the staff lived on the ranch, most of the house staff on the third floor, although Sam had a "small apartment" behind the kitchen.

Right about then, two younger girls, probably both in their late teens and aproned in light blue, like Sam, entered the kitchen. They stopped their giggling when they spotted Slocum, and Sam introduced them to him.

"Mornin', Zelda and Mary," he said, nodding his head slightly in acknowledgment. Zelda was blond and Mary was brunette, and he recognized them as two of the table servants who had hovered behind them at the evening meals, seeing to the coffee and the course changes.

Both curtsied, then scurried off to the dining room to get the table ready.

He hoped that if Xander had any thoughts of easing his loins in the near future, it would be with one of them. He'd already marked Samantha for himself. He couldn't help but admire her tiny waist, lush bosom, and fine ankles, which flashed with the movement of her skirts as she worked around the kitchen. She took a pot of oatmeal off the stove and emptied it into a serving dish, then removed her third tray of toast from the oven, emptied it, and filled another.

"Mary?" she called out, and the girl appeared in the doorway. "Would you please slice the ham?"

Mary obediently brought the ham to the table and began cutting thick slices, which Sam took and placed in her big frying pan. "Do you think you'll be back for lunch, Slocum, or should I fix you and Xander something to take along?"

"Take along, if it ain't too much trouble," he replied.

In the end, she prepared, wrapped, and packed four thick, fried ham sandwiches, two large servings of fried potatoes, two thick wedges of last night's dried apple pie, and a large thermos of hot coffee.

"Xander's gonna be in hog heaven," he said with a grin when he took the parcel from her. "Thanks!"

"My pleasure," she said, smiling as the first sleepy voices sounded in the dining room. Mary and Zelda scurried back and forth, carrying fresh butter, salt and pepper, and platters of pancakes and eggs and sausage.

"Zelda, take that package from Mr. Slocum and put it on the table in the front hallway, would you please?" Sam said just as two footmen came in the kitchen's back door, one adjusting his gloves. Neither could be older than twenty. "Mr. Slocum," she said, obviously reserving the honor of the dropped "Mister" for herself, "meet our two footmen and my brothers, Nils and Thor."

Both young men bowed, saying, "Mr. Slocum, sir."

Slocum didn't know what to say, so he said, "Mornin', fellas," and hoped it was proper enough.

He supposed it was, because both boys grinned at him before they took off for the dining room to pour coffee.

Slocum wisely decided to go with them. "It's been a true pleasure, Miss Sam," he said before he exited. "I really mean that."

She smiled, and tried to hide the fact that her eyes briefly flicked toward his crotch when he rose.

She was interested, too. Inside, Slocum was so excited that he wanted to yodel. But instead, he nodded at her, grinning, then went to the door.

"Come to my kitchen anytime, Slocum," she said, those pale blue eyes twinkling. "Anytime at all."

Mumbling his thanks, Slocum went into the dining room and sat in his chair, shaking his head. He was almost blushing!

9

Conversation around the breakfast table was limited that morning, to say the least. Only Hiram had anything to say, and most of it was worthless chatter as usual. Slocum silently ate his breakfast, which consisted of flapjacks with honey, a handful of bacon strips, and black coffee. He reminded himself to tell Xander to bring his own sugar when they set out. Sam had put nothing but coffee in the thermos.

They were just standing up—and Goose was still eyeing Slocum—when there came a knock at the front door.

It was the boy who'd been sent into Tucson yesterday, the boy who'd sent the telegrams, and who had been waiting for replies. Apparently, he'd received them.

Slocum waved him over to Goose, who eagerly took the papers and one at a time, ripped them open. He stared at them a long time. Even Hiram was silent, waiting and wondering, along with the rest of them, whether Goose's next action would be to pull his gun or to apologize.

It was neither. He slowly looked up from the papers in

his hands and said, "How do I know you didn't pay these fellers off? How do I know they ain't lyin' for you?"

Slocum imperceptibly gave his head a shake. Just like he'd figured, a building would have to fall on top of Goose before he'd let this cockeyed notion go. He said, "Who has to drop an anvil on you anyhow? Did you list those dates? Did they confirm 'em?"

After what seemed like five long minutes, Goose finally shook his head. "They did," he said.

Beside Slocum, Xander let out an enormous sigh of relief, and even Hiram allowed himself to slouch a bit. Slocum couldn't help but be a little surprised that Hiram had even noticed anything of importance was transpiring.

Hiram spoke, the corners of his mouth turning up and his tone jovial. "Well, good! Wonderful! Wonderful news, Goose!"

Goose didn't look as though the news was "wonderful" at all, but he nodded quickly to acknowledge Hiram's speech. Xander tried to change the subject by crossing to the table at the center of the entryway and picking up the parcel there. "What's this?" he asked.

Slocum quickly glanced over. "Our lunch. Treat it kindly."

Xander carefully set the parcel back down. "Are we goin' out today? Gonna catch those rustlers?"

Slocum said, "God willin'. Goose, you wanna tag along? We could use a good man with a gun."

Goose looked thunderstruck. "You want me along? You want me along when I could still be holdin' a grudge against you, when I might plug you in the back or worse?"

Slocum shrugged. "Seems to me you've got proof to the contrary there in your hand. I don't think you're stupid, Goose. I don't believe a stupid man could have tracked me and Xander down here. But I figure a smart man would take me up on that offer to help him ferret out the real killer. That offer still stands."

Goose stood mute for a moment, the wheels behind his eyes silently turning, before he spoke. "All right. I'll go."

"Good enough," said Slocum. "Xander, get the package. Let's go get the horses tacked up and ready."

Speck was ready and eager to be on the move, and Slocum let him canter for the first mile or so before he slowed him down to a jog. He'd only had the gelding for a few months, but Speck was still thick with muscle from the hard work he'd done before Slocum got his hands on him.

He'd been used to haul logs down off a mountainside— by dragging them, not hauling them on a wagon. But that obviously wasn't where he'd started out. Somebody had done a good bit of training on the Appy to make him as cow-smart as he was. And after hauling all those logs down a mountainside, he was always full of piss and vinegar, always willing to do more than Slocum could ask of him.

Xander's sorrel Appy, Eagle, was some younger than Speck, but looked to be a good horse, too. He needed some finishing work, but then, so did Xander. Slocum smiled. A couple of green-broke youngsters were what he'd inherited. Green as saplings, but ready to be turned into mighty oaks.

He turned his attention to Goose, who was riding his black bay gelding about twenty yards off Slocum's left shoulder. He knew that Goose was still having misgivings about those telegrams. He knew Goose was going over every possibility, trying to figure how Slocum could have interfered with those telegrams or interfered with their authors.

But Slocum knew Goose was going to run up against a

brick wall every time, unless he came up with some possibility that Slocum hadn't figured on. If Goose was going to kill him, it would have to be out of outright meanness. And Slocum didn't think he had it in him. He figured he and Goose were too much alike. Same height, same build, and features close enough alike that people could mistake them for brothers, Slocum thought. There was even a trace of the South still lingering on Goose's tongue. He couldn't make out where Goose had come from originally, but it was someplace around Alabama, maybe Georgia. But his proficiency with that horse of his pointed to a life lived in the saddle.

Slocum shrugged. It was none of his business really.

Around noon, the slit in the mesa wall was getting big enough to see, and Slocum called a halt. "Let's stop out here and have some lunch where we can water the horses." He waved a hand to the right, where Xander's horse was already drinking.

Goose, who seemed to have calmed down considerably since morning, nodded and slid off his mount, then led him toward the water, followed by Slocum and Speck.

All three horses having had their fill, the three men sat down in the shade of the few cottonwoods that grew beside the little spring, and hauled out Sam's vittles. It seemed that Sam had been holding out on Goose, because he produced a smaller package—she'd made lunch for Goose, too.

By the time Slocum and company reached the opening to the box canyon, nothing had changed. The brush was still where they'd piled it, and no new tracks made by riders pocked the canyon floor. Slocum took a ride into the box canyon where the stock had been held, and found nothing changed—except for a fresh bale of hay, probably tossed down during the night. Which meant that the rustlers were on to them.

Swearing under his breath, Slocum exited the box canyon and rode out to wave in the other two riders. When he explained what had happened, Xander let loose with a snarling "Damn it, anyway!" and smacked his hat across his knee.

Goose, looking very disappointed, grumbled under his breath, then asked, "There's another way up there?" He pointed toward the canyon's rim.

Slocum nodded. "They been dumping hay and water over the side of the south rim."

"Get up there with a wagon?"

"Yup."

"Well, seems to me three men on horseback ought to be able to manage it then," said Goose.

Slocum wanted to clap him on the back, but he was too far away. So he said, "Right you are, Goose. So which is it, boys? Do we go clear back to Hiram's and ease up onto the mesa that way, or do we finish cutting through and hope there's something closer on the south side?"

"Cut through," said Goose and Xander in unison. Xander laughed, and the corners of Goose's mouth quirked up.

"All right," said Slocum, who couldn't help but smile, too, especially at Goose. He was going to be fine after all. "Let's go!"

And they headed down the canyon, still all grinning, but still on the alert for the sounds or signs of any other traveler.

When Milo Herrick awoke that morning, he didn't bother to stop and tell the other hands, who had come in late last night after playing poker and messing with women in Tucson. No, he rolled straight out of bed and fairly ran up to the main house.

It wasn't nearly as grand as Hiram Walker's place, or even as nice as Cord Whipple's. It was only four rooms, but they were nice ones, and Milo figured any hand worth his salt—any hand who told the truth, that is—would have traded places with Smollets any day.

As he had last night, he banged on the door. This morning, Harvey Smollets himself answered it, looking like he'd just climbed out of bed and wasn't any too happy about it.

Before Smollets had a chance to open his mouth, Milo began. "They're gone, Mr. Smollets! I went to feed 'em last night like always, and they were just plain gone! The brush was all pulled down from the way in, and the cows had vamoosed!"

Harvey Smollets, who had listened to Milo's rant with his jaw hanging open, closed it with a click of his teeth. He blinked. "What?"

Milo repeated himself, nearly word for word, and waited.

He didn't have to wait long. Smollets stepped to the side, to the big triangle hanging from the roof beams, and began to ring it loud and hard. So loud, in fact, that for the last of it Milo had to put his hands over his ears to keep them from splitting!

And then the hands—all three of them—boiled up from the bunkhouse.

When they were all standing there, panting, in a row, Smollets turned to Milo and said, "Tell them what you told me."

Once again, Milo repeated the story, word for word. Immediately, he felt as if he were being bombarded with stupid questions.

"What time was it?"

"Who took our brush down?"

"Were they *all* gone, all twenty-five of 'em?"

"Where'd they take off to, Milo?"

Finally, Milo sank down to his knees and angled both arms over his head while he shouted, "I don't know! I'm tellin' you, I don't know and nobody was here when I come back in! I didn't know what to do and I still don't! Mr. Smollets, what should I do?"

10

Slocum, Goose, and Xander continued through the canyon, stopping occasionally to rest the horses, and finally exited the passage through a narrow slot. This deposited them on the southern side of the mesa's base—and still there were no tracks.

This came as a surprise to Slocum, who had expected to find the rustlers had abandoned their brush drag not far past the opening to the box canyon. Goose, too, seemed perplexed. "Somebody wanna tell me what them sonsabitches did? Did the Good Lord just lift 'em up to Heaven?"

Slocum snorted. "If the Lord had anything to do with it, I reckon they'd be goin' the other way."

Goose smiled, then looked out farther to the south, where Xander was zigzagging through the brush, searching for sign. "That's a good boy you've got there," he observed.

"Yup," Slocum said. Although he was thinking, *He might just as easily be yours.* He sat there for a moment thinking, and then he said something he hadn't expected to say. "Goose, you ever been in Texas? Down to El Paso?"

Goose saw nothing odd in the question, and replied, "Yeah, a few times. Why? That where you're from?"

Slocum shook his head. "Nope. It's where Xander's from originally, though."

Goose didn't speak, just nodded, and Slocum sat there for a few minutes more, trying to decide what to do. At last, he said, "Goose, did you know a gal named Cissy Carter, used to work down at the Crystal Slipper?"

Goose's face lit up like Christmas morning. "Hell, ol' Cissy? Man, I haven't heard that name in forever! Yes, I know her. Or I knew her. She was one fine piece of . . . she was one fine gal." And then his brow furrowed a bit. "Why you askin'? Nothin' wrong with her, is there?"

Slocum glanced out ahead. Xander was farther off than before, still combing the ground.

Slocum said, "She's dead, Goose." As a single tear began to slowly work its way down Goose's weather-beaten cheek, Slocum added, "And she's Xander's mother."

Goose's head jerked up at that, and the tear flew off his face. "Cissy's boy? Cissy had a boy? With *you*?"

"Don't look so damn thunderstruck," Slocum growled. "When's the last time you saw her?"

Goose scratched at his earlobe. "Quite a while, quite a while . . . Must be seventeen years now. Eighteen come next January. Ain't it funny how a woman can stay with you that long, even when she's not around?"

"Yeah," muttered Slocum. "Real funny." There wasn't a trace of a smile on his face. Now what should he do? He had gradually come to accept that Xander was his boy. He was getting to like it. But he had once wondered if Cissy had a liking for a particular type of man—Irish, and looking to be moving on—and it seemed he was right. Goose must have been in town right before him. Cissy must have already been pregnant when Slocum had bedded her, although it would have been far too soon for her to tell.

So, what did he do now? He could forget any of this ever happened. He could just keep his mouth shut and not tell Xander or Goose. After all, a man couldn't suffer over something he knew nothing about. And it was *possible* that Xander was his son, wasn't it?

But when it came down to the important things in life, Slocum was as honest as they came. And he knew. He supposed he'd known all along, damn it.

But knowing something and saying it were two very different things. He couldn't just blurt it out. Not to Goose, who'd think he was out of his mind. And not to Xander, who'd been told he was a Slocum every day of his life. It bore further thought before he went around telling everybody, he decided.

Just in time, too, because Xander came galloping up to them. "I finally found tracks!" he shouted gleefully.

Slocum and Goose needed no further inspiration. They both clucked to their mounts and headed toward the place that Xander had indicated, sweeping him up in their wake.

It didn't take them long to reach the place. It was about forty yards to the south of where he and Goose had been waiting. Suddenly, the tracks of two shod horses just magically appeared. Over to one side and tossed carelessly atop some live sage, Slocum spotted what had been left of their drag, tattered and practically leafless.

He pointed. "There's the drag."

Goose nodded. "Tracks head southeast."

Slocum said, "You up to it?"

"Don't see why not." Goose looked toward the boy. "Hey, kid!"

Xander looked up at Goose.

"You wanna go round up some cattle rustlers?"

Slocum watched as Xander's grin widened. It was all still a big, wide, wonderful adventure for the kid, wasn't it? Every cloud had a silver lining, and there was a fat pot of gold at the end of every rainbow.

"Can we, Pa?" Xander was looking toward him eagerly.

Slocum had to turn his head. He couldn't look at the boy, now that he knew the truth of the matter. Raggedly, he nodded, giving his affirmation.

Xander gave a hoot, and Goose and he barreled ahead, hot on the trail. Roughly, Slocum rubbed at his eyes with his fist, grumbled, "Aw, hell!" and from a standing start, pushed Speck into a lope. He followed the others.

Harvey Smollets stood there a few moments, staring at young Milo Herrick and trying to decide what was better: to whip the boy for the cattle loss, which was obviously not his fault—although he certainly would make a handy scapegoat, and it would make Smollets feel better—or to just accept the loss of stock and move on to the next target.

He decided.

"It is not your fault, Milo," he began, and the boy practically melted into the ground with relief. Smollets turned toward the handful of others standing there waiting, and said, "How far out did you drag the brush?"

"Almost a quarter mile, Mr. Smollets," said Roy.

"And you followed the usual pattern?"

"Yessir!" came the reply.

Then once again, Smollets fell silent. He pinched his chin between thumb and forefinger, thinking.

"Mr. Smollets, sir?" said Roy. "What you want we should do next?"

Smollets, hand still on his chin, said, "Nothing. Forget those few head. Forget you were ever on the Walking W. Chip?"

A hand with shaggy blond hair snapped to attention. Smollets ran a tight ship. "Yessir, Mr. Smollets?"

"I want you and Milo to go out and make certain that those tracks are obliterated. Gone. Vanished. The rest of you, return to your duties."

All at once, the hands said, "Yessir!" and broke up their little knot to carry out their orders. He noticed Roy sliding a curious glance toward Milo, but Milo was too busy hurrying toward the barn and the horses to notice. He was right not to have struck the boy, he thought. Good hands were hard to find; loyal hands, even harder.

"And all of you, stay clear of Cord Whipple's place. He's noticed the hay," he snapped before he turned around, walked back up the porch steps, and kicked the adobe wall as hard as he could, chipping its brittle surface.

"Any port in a storm," he muttered, and went inside to find his pipe.

Out on the range, Slocum had lost the trail. The tracks had wandered into an area that was rocky and hard and didn't take tracks, and he and his companions had been trying to find the trail again for the past hour. They were currently fanned out over a wide valley, and it didn't look like anybody was having any luck.

Slocum pulled his horse up, rested one hand on the saddle horn, and stuck two fingers of his spare hand in his mouth, whistling up Xander. He waved the boy in, then signaled in the opposite direction for Goose. As the riders came trotting in, he slid off Speck, patting his neck.

"You think we've looked enough for one day, Speck?" Slocum asked, then shook his head. "Naw, you'd prob'ly keep goin' till you couldn't stand up anymore. Hell, you'd likely crawl after 'em on your belly!"

"Talkin' to yourself?" asked Goose, who was the first one in. "Gonna stop here for the night?" When Slocum nodded, Goose continued. "Good. Been thinkin' favorable 'bout some outta-the-saddle sittin'."

"What's that?" asked Xander, riding in. He cocked his head at both Slocum and Goose, who were loosening the girths of both their saddles. "Are we stoppin' already?"

He looked disappointed.

"Sun's almost down," said Slocum.

"I got extra food if anybody needs it," said Goose.

Reluctantly, Xander slid from his horse.

It turned out that Slocum and Goose had remarkably similar thoughts on how to set up a camp, so it was completed in no time. Xander's job was to get the horses settled in, which he did to both Goose's and Slocum's satisfaction. Between the three of them, they had enough food for supper with a little left over, which Slocum had Xander put away for their breakfast.

Xander was still complaining about the halt, even though it was all the way dark by the time they put dinner away. Slocum said, "You couldn't see a damn thing over there now even if you were carryin' a torch!"

"But I thought I found the trace of a hoofprint just off the rock!"

Slocum nodded. "It'll still be there come mornin'. I promise, we'll go over there first thing and look for it. All right?"

When the boy didn't answer right away, Goose piped up, "We'll all go, kid, okay?"

At last, Xander said, "Okay." But he sort of grumbled the answer. Slocum shook his head. He'd expect any boy of his to mind him better. But then he reminded himself—Xander wasn't really his, was he?

Should he tell Goose tonight? He glanced over. Goose was leaning back against a big rock, staring up at the stars. And Xander's head was already nodding. In a few minutes, his chin would be on his chest and he'd be out like a light.

So much for the bravery of Slocum! As he stretched out within the confines of his lariat, following Xander's example, Slocum thought that perhaps tomorrow might be a better day for it. And that he was a coward and a jackass for not just saying it out and getting it over with.

But the truth was that he enjoyed playing the part of the papa. It wasn't his fault that Cissy had thought wrong about it. It wasn't his fault that the kid had seemingly read everything ever published about him. And most of all, it wasn't his fault that secretly, he really wanted Xander to be his boy. He wanted to have someone to carry on his name, someone to give him grandchildren, someone to mourn him when he was gone.

But it wasn't to be. Xander wasn't his. That much was clear now anyway. He rolled over to face Goose, determined to open up a conversation with him, but when he finally rolled over enough to see him, Goose was dead to the world.

He looked at Xander again. Same thing. They even slept

alike; their heads cocked to one side, their mouths hanging open.

Grunting, Slocum turned back over and went to sleep, vowing to say something to them tomorrow. Goose first, he thought. Then, Goose could tell Xander.

Slocum couldn't.

11

Back at the Walking W, Hiram had finished another huge dinner, had his brandy, and gone off to bed. Down in the kitchen, Mary and Zelda, the kitchen maids, were finishing up the last of the supper dishes. This was a good thing, because Zelda was about to nod off. Her head fell gently on Mary's shoulder every few minutes, and Mary none too gently shrugged her off.

Samantha sat at the big kitchen table with her brothers, Nils and Thor, who were playing cards. Sam herself was seated at the head of the table, snapping beans for tomorrow's lunch—and wishing that Slocum would ride back in. She'd been disappointed this afternoon, and she supposed she'd be disappointed for at least part of tomorrow, too.

She kept on snapping beans, not looking up despite the fact that one of her brothers had just spoken to her. "What was that, Thor?"

"It was Nils," said Thor.

"All right. What did you say, Nils?"

"I asked you when your boyfriend was getting back."

Sam finally lifted her head. "My boyfriend? Who on earth—?"

Nils made a face at her. "We all see the way you look at Slocum."

Sam rolled her eyes. Brothers could be so annoying! She said, "How can you see me looking at him? He isn't even here."

Thor got into the conversation. "Yeah, but he was here yesterday and this morning, and before that, too."

Sam shook her head. "If you two are so bored that Mr. Slocum is the only thing you have to worry about, maybe you oughta clean out the cellar." She smiled into her beans.

Snap snap snap . . .

Nils grumbled, "Aw, forget it. Every time we find somethin' to rib her about, she says to clean out the cellar!"

Thor, the older of the two, said, "That's 'cause she's the cook and we're lowly footmen."

"That's right," Sam said with a nod of her head. "You'd best remember that, Nils." Although the words were stern, her voice was playful and she smiled a little into her lap. She glanced over toward the sink, and saw Zelda starting to nod off again. "One of you fellows had best get to the sink and catch Zelda before she falls."

Both boys shot to their feet and managed to catch Zelda halfway to the floor. They helped the groggy girl to her feet and Nils asked her, "How come you're so sleepy all the time this past week?"

Zelda looked at him, then Thor, then Nils again. "Dunno. Just tired, I reckon."

Nils grumbled, "Seems to me a body ought to have a reason, no matter how lame it is . . ."

Zelda shook herself free of the boys' arms. "I said I was just tired, all right? Let me go!"

Both boys took a step backward.

To Samantha, who found all of this quite curious, Zelda said, "Can I go to my quarters now?"

Sam nodded. "Good night. See you at breakfast."

Answering with a quick "Night," Zelda went out the back door to the service hall. Sam heard her shoes clicking on the treads as she went up the back stairs.

"Thor?" she said in a conversational tone.

"What?"

"Anything you want to tell me about Zelda? I'm likely to be a lot more forgiving than Daddy."

Thor appeared thunderstruck. Had she read his mind? But Sam was simply his older sister and, having known him all his life, knew him pretty well. He slumped down in a chair at the table and heaved a heavy sigh.

He said, "No, nothin'."

"Don't try to fool me, Thor," she said kindly. "You might get away with it with anybody else, but not your sister." She reached out and put a soft hand on his forearm. "You know what's wrong with Zelda, don't you?"

He dropped his head, but he didn't pull away from her. A good sign. He muttered, "Yeah, Sam. We been . . . we been keeping company."

He stopped, but she urged him on. "And?" she said softly.

His head drooped even farther. "And she's with child. My child. She's about a month and a half along. Guess that's why she's so tired all the time." Slowly, he raised his head. "Sam, I'm sorry. I'm sorry I brought this shame on you and Daddy and all the others. I'm just plain sorry."

"Do you love her?"

He nodded. "With all of my heart. I wanna marry her, but she keeps sayin' no."

This seemed odd, and Sam asked, "Why?"

"She says not only would my daddy be mad, hers would skin her alive. I told her that havin' a baby with no husband around would get her *whupped* and skinned, but she says that's a long way off."

Sam slowly shook her head. Zelda was only fifteen to Thor's sixteen, but she supposed seven and a half months probably seemed years away when you were that young. Sam, at twenty-two, liked to think she'd gained a little experience in her old age.

"Don't worry, baby," she said. "I'll talk to Zelda about it. The circuit rider's coming next Wednesday, and he can marry you, make everything nice and legal, all right?"

An anvil seemed to have been lifted off Thor's shoulders, and he looked her in the eye. "Really? You think you could talk her into it?"

"I do, little brother."

Tears of relief were welling in Thor's blue eyes, and childlike, he suddenly lurched across the table and kissed her on the cheek. "Thanks, Samantha. Thanks so dang much . . ."

She patted him, saying, "It's all right, Thor. It'll be all right. And you and Zelda are going to live a long and happy life together." She smiled. "Or else!"

"Thank you, Sam," he repeated over and over, "thank you so much."

She playfully pushed him away. "All right now. Go on to bed and get some sleep, or I'll skin you alive."

He stood up, grinning, and said, "Yes, ma'am!"

He went on out the service door to the back stairs, and

suddenly Sam realized she wasn't alone. Mary was still at the sink, drying the last of the dishes, and Nils leaned against the counter on the other side of the room.

Nils was the first to speak. "Get it settled? You gonna turn him in to Papa?"

Sam was fairly certain he couldn't have heard much, but he likely already knew, since he and Thor roomed together. She said, "Problem's taken care of," adding to herself, *Except for a few minor details, like getting the bride to be to agree to the whole thing.*

Nils grinned. "Great! Thanks, sis."

She waved him off. "Oh, go to bed."

"Right." He turned back toward the sink. "Night, Mary."

It was obvious that Mary was clueless to the situation. Nils's words made her jump, and she said, "What?"

"Nothing, Mary," said Sam with a smile. "Why don't you go on up to bed, too? I'll finish up drying those pots for you."

Slocum was having a nice dream—it was about Sam, and it was just starting to get interesting—when somebody shook him awake. Without thinking, he reached for his Colt, and just about shot Xander in the face.

"Christ, boy! Don't go 'round waking up fellas sudden like that!" he groused.

Xander didn't react to Slocum's censure, but instead hissed, "Riders!" and pointed out across the valley.

Sure enough, once he sat up, Slocum could make out two riders who were dragging a chunk of brush behind them along the ground. Distantly, he could hear its soft rustle and thump. He flicked a glance toward where they'd had their fire. Thank God it had burnt out some time ago, and appeared to be cold. And the riders didn't appear to know there was anyone else in the valley. He heard the soft rumble of casual conversation, but couldn't make out any words.

Xander started to stand up, to get to his feet, but Slocum quickly pulled him back down, hissing, "Keep low. They ain't seen us yet, and I'm hopin' to go on just the same way."

Their horses had been quiet so far, but the animals were making a dent in the skyline, Slocum knew. But he also knew there was a low range of hills in the distance behind them. He hoped that any ears that stuck up over its black form would go unnoticed.

He and Xander watched the riders for the next half hour as they seemed to carefully go over the ground—and their own just-laid tracks—with the drag. They never made it back as far as the place where Xander was so sure he'd seen something, but they did a good job of it, so far as Slocum could tell.

When they finally finished and began to ride slowly away, still pulling the drag behind them, Slocum put his hand on Xander's arm to get his attention. "Go wake up Goose. Gently," he added as a reminder.

He must've done it right, because Goose came awake without so much as a grouch or a grumble. Slocum motioned him over and pointed to the retreating riders, then explained what he planned to do.

"You're joshin'," said Goose when Slocum had finished. Even Xander looked a tad befuddled.

"If we just let them go, we don't know which way they're headed once they're outta the line of sight," Slocum said patiently. "This way, if we travel soft, we can follow 'em all the way back to wherever the hell it is they're goin'."

Goose stood up. "It's your party, I reckon," he said, and began to gather up his gear.

Slocum, too, got to his feet and started grabbing his blanket and saddlebags. "C'mon, Xander, you, too. And by the way, nice work."

"Huh?"

Slocum rephrased the compliment. "That was real good, you seein' those boys and figuring out what they were up to."

"Oh!" The kid's face lit up. "Thanks, Pa!"

Goddamn it, there he went with that "Pa" stuff again. Slocum was half tempted to sit him and Goose down right then and there, but a glance at the eastern horizon told him he'd best get going or he'd lose his prey. He was fast losing sight of the riders.

Quickly, they packed up again and resaddled the horses and rode out to the east. The riders had gone by then, but Slocum had imprinted their last appearance on the horizon in his brain, and led Goose and Xander straight to the place. There, they had to move quickly across a small ridge lest they be seen.

Goose spotted the riders first.

"Over there," he said quietly, pointing to the southeast.

Slocum squinted, then saw them. "Good catch," he said, and pushed Speck the rest of the way down the slope of the ridge.

"My pleasure," replied Goose with a grin. "You know, it ain't as bad goin' out here as I thought."

"Long as the moon holds out," Slocum said with a nod. Indeed, the moon that lit their way was still partly full and clear of clouds. It didn't look like it'd be covered by clouds anytime soon. Actually, it didn't look like it would be covered by clouds ever.

But Slocum knew this wasn't true. It was coming time for the summer wets, also called the monsoons, and at the drop of a hat, a thunderstorm, rainstorm, or windstorm—sometimes all three at once—could blow up, seemingly out of nowhere, to flatten the countryside.

12

Slocum wished that he hadn't thought about the weather, because at that moment he found himself, Xander, and Goose huddled at the edge of a rock outcrop, their horses pulled close with their butts to the whipping wind, while hard rain pelted them all. Brush, and even limbs from trees, flew across the desert, striking the horses and making them kick out and pull at their handlers.

Xander was beginning to tire, and Slocum took his horse's reins away. Now fighting two horses who wanted to get out of there in the worst way, he said, shouting over the howling wind, "Sit down, Xander. Take a break."

The boy needed no coaxing. He slid his back down along the surface of rock behind him, and plopped into a sit. His head immediately fell to his chest. In the flashes of lightning that followed, Slocum could tell he'd fallen asleep.

"Whoa, Kip! Easy, boy!" Goose said beside him. The gelding had just been hit broadside by almost a whole clump of sage, and hadn't liked it one bit. He pulled away from Goose and up, half rearing and pulling the big man off his feet.

Quickly, Slocum slipped Speck's reins to his left hand so that he could grab the back of Goose's shirt, hauling him back to earth. "Thanks, pal," Goose said loudly once he had Kip back under control.

"Welcome," Slocum shouted. *Was now the time?* he wondered. Xander was out like the proverbial light. But the circumstances were far from relaxed.

No, he decided. *Be patient. Its time'll come.*

As it turned out, he made the right decision because shortly thereafter, perhaps not even five minutes later, the storm quite suddenly stopped. Slocum watched its edge move away from them, toward the north, like a yellowed gray wall.

"Whew," he muttered.

"No kiddin'," Goose replied. "You in Arizona a lot of the time?"

"As much as I'm anywhere."

"They get these turd floaters all the time?"

Now he sounded like he came from West Texas. Slocum gave up on trying to figure him out. He said, "Come about the middle of July, yeah. They last till about the end of August. It's what they call a monsoon."

"Figures they'd have a name for it," said Goose with a droplet-scattering shake of his head. He'd taken off his hat in order to scrub his face with his bandanna. His hair, normally sandy red and pale with the gray mixed in, looked a lot more reddish when it was wet, although Slocum didn't have long to look. Goose slapped his hat right back on and leaned back against the wall of stone.

Slocum stepped away from the rock, walking the horses

in circles while he checked their legs for any permanent damage that might have been done by flying debris. Thank God, both horses looked fit, if they were still a little spooked. Eagle was the worst, continually craning his head one way and another, looking for the next stick or rock to fly at him. Speck, a bit more even-tempered—and a bit older—seemed to take it all in stride.

But Slocum himself felt like a drowned rat. He was soaked through and dead tired. And pissed off. They'd had to gallop through the storm to get to the shelter of the rocks, and in the process, had lost track of the cowboys they were trailing. Goose didn't seem to care, and Xander was asleep with his butt in a mud puddle.

Slocum led the horses back to the rock and slouched against it, next to Goose.

"They okay?" Goose muttered groggily.

"Seem to be," Slocum replied. "You too tired to keep ridin'?"

"That's a big yessir, Cap'n," Goose said. His horse nuzzled him in seeming agreement. "I'm all for campin' on the spot and catchin' a little shut-eye." He glanced down at Xander. "Seems like your 'monsoons' wear a feller out!"

Slocum wearily nodded. He was too tired to go on, too, but Goose and Xander gave him a nice excuse. "We'll get up at dawn, try to pick up their trail again, all right?"

Goose nodded curtly. "Sounds fine to me." He stepped out into the open and began unsaddling his horse. "Gonna be hard to find any dry ground to pull up."

Slocum began unsaddling Speck. "Downright impossible."

"Let's stay here, tie the ponies to that ol' stump, and lie on the blankets."

It was just what Slocum had been thinking, and he nodded his agreement. "We best get the boy up out of the water after we've got things set."

Goose grunted his affirmation, and they proceeded to set up camp.

Slocum figured it was a good thing that they didn't start a campfire, there being no dry wood anywhere about, because the same storm that hit them would have also hit the rustlers, and sent them scurrying for cover, too. He wouldn't be surprised to find them camped within his range of vision.

At least, he hoped that would be the case.

He and Goose finished spreading the blankets, including the kid's, and while Goose looped the sleeping area with rope, in case of snakes, Slocum roused Xander enough to get him moved to the blankets. The second the kid had moved, he stretched out and was sleeping again. Slocum covered him with his saddle blanket. The storm had really cooled everything off—for now. Right now, it was chilly, but Slocum knew it'd be miserable in the morning: hot and humid.

Hot and humid didn't half describe it. The morning dawned hazy, the air thick enough to cut with a table knife, and by eight or so, they were steaming in their still-wet clothes. The horses were sweating, their necks and flanks heavy with it, despite the fact that they were keeping to a walk or a slow jog.

At least Slocum had been right about the riders they were trailing. It took less than ten minutes to spot their slowly moving shapes, and they'd been tracking them ever since, pausing only to rest the horses when Slocum or Goose figured they might be seen.

"Y'know," said Slocum as he rocked lazily in the saddle,

"I don't believe these boys are goin' back to any ranch. They're headed straight for Tucson, unless I miss my guess."

"Reckon I'll have to side with you, since I don't know where the hell Tucson is from here," Goose said. "Or from anywhere. I only been to Arizona a couple times, and that was just to cross it. And one'a them times was by train."

Xander perked up at that. "You rode a train all the way across Arizona?"

Goose grinned, tickled at his enthusiasm. "All across New Mexico, too, and part of California."

"Across states _and_ territories?" the boy practically shouted.

"You end up in Texas?" Slocum asked, guessing that his last stop was El Paso.

"Matter of fact, it was," Goose replied, winking at Slocum. "They'd just built the railroad on the old Mormon Trail then. That's across the southern part of Arizona, kid. I may not be much of a dry land navigator, but I remember what I've read or been told. 'Specially if it's interesting," he added with a grin.

Xander was like a dog with a bone. "What's it like, speedin' over the countryside?"

"You mean you ain't never been on a train, kid?" Goose turned to Slocum. "You been neglectin' this kid's education! You been on a train?"

Slocum nodded. "Just this last year. Went from Sacramento down to . . . what's the name of that scruffy little town? Oh, yeah. Los Angeles."

Xander twisted toward him. "You been on a train, too, Pa?" His eyes were wide, as if he could scarcely believe he was in the company of two such seasoned and worldly travelers.

"Slocum, you been half the length of California without takin' your son along?" Goose appeared confused.

It was now or never, Slocum figured. So he just said it as plain as he could. "Didn't know I had a son until a week or so ago."

Goose looked mad, then curiosity played at the corners of his eyes. "You didn't?"

"I found him!" Xander said happily.

"Cissy was his ma," Slocum continued, without turning toward Xander. "I figure I must've rode into town right after you rode out."

Suddenly, Goose pulled up his horse. "Say *what*?"

Slocum said, "You heard me. Anybody owes this fine boy a ride on a train, it isn't me, sorry to say."

Xander, who had ridden on a bit ahead, turned Eagle around and came back looking puzzled. "I don't understand," was all he said. He looked at Slocum, then Goose, then back again. "What's goin' on?"

Goose looked too thunderstruck to reply, so Slocum said, "Xander, I been calculatin', and it hurts me to say it, but I think Cissy guessed wrong in thinkin' I was your daddy."

"But—"

Softly, Goose said, "You don't have to look far to see him, Xander. Look at your hair color. Look at the way you act. I seen you back there, the way you scout around on a horse and the way you eat peaches—on a knife's tip, straight out of the can."

"You sleep alike, too," Slocum added. "Heads tipped to the left and your mouths open. And the resemblance? It's unquietin'."

Xander tipped his head up. "All right, which of you has the birthmark? Ma never said Slocum had one, but . . ."

Slocum had no birthmarks, only scars from a hundred different bullets, arrows, knives, and Indian lances. But Goose looked up and tugged at his collar. "Like this?"

A small mark, shaped like a profiled moth at rest, rode his collar bone.

Xander's eyes bugged out and he began to tear at the buttons of his collar. "I got the same!" he shouted. The mark was nearly identical, and he was breathing hard.

Slocum shook his head. "Well, I'm as sad to hear it as I am happy for you two fellers. The Good Lord sure works in mysterious ways, don't he?"

Goose was down off his horse and practically caught Xander in midair. They clapped each other on the back over and over, saying all sorts of things that Slocum didn't want to hear, and so he rode Speck about twenty feet over to one side.

Xander and Goose didn't notice.

From his new vantage point, Slocum spotted the riders ahead once again. Riding at a slow pace, they were indeed headed for the outskirts of Tucson. Slocum sat there a few moments, torn between silently lamenting the loss of Xander—if anybody was going to have a kid, it should have been a kid like Xander—and wishing he could just lasso those two boys down below before they got all the way into town.

But he couldn't even set out at a gallop. Xander and his pa were still thumping and pounding and crying—it was strange to see big old Goose cry—and carrying on, so he waited until they were done.

Which took exactly a half hour.

Slocum wouldn't have noticed, except for Xander walking up to his horse and motioning him down. When he dismounted, Xander unexpectedly threw his arms around

Slocum, and said, "I was awful pleased to have you for my pa while it lasted. You're a good man."

Slocum extricated himself from the kid, holding him at arm's length. "That goes for me, too, Xander. Havin' you for a son was an honor. And it's not like we ain't never gonna see each other again. We still got these rustlers to round up, and then we gotta find this killer that Goose is lookin' for and get that set straight."

Xander looked him in the eye. "You just go from one adventure to the next, don't you?"

His brow arched, Slocum nodded. "Never thought about it, but yeah. Guess I do."

13

Samantha, having talked at length with Zelda—and having made her see sense—relayed the welcome news of his pending nuptials to her brother, Thor. Now, she stood at one of the kitchen windows, watching the two of them talk out by the water pump. She smiled. They really did look like a couple in love.

Just as well. Barring flood and famine—and any one of the premature fates that could strike a person out here in the Territories—they would remain a couple for at least fifty years.

Sam left the window and turned toward the table, where she was preparing Mr. Walker's lunch. She hoped it would be only him, but you never could tell—she cooked for four, just in case. Any leftovers could be used at supper or breakfast, if not during one or two of Mr. Walker's frequent "hunger attacks."

The peach pie she'd been baking was ready to come out,

and she tended to it. "Mary?" she said. "Could you shout for Zelda? I think we're going to need her."

"'Bout time," she heard Mary grumble as she went out the door. Samantha smiled. Mary was young—just turned fourteen, although she looked older—and she was jealous of the feelings Thor and Zelda had for one another. Well, her time would come. Although, hopefully with somebody else's brother. There was something about that girl that didn't sit quite right with Sam, although if asked for an explanation, she'd be stumped for an answer.

As she began to cut the chicken she'd plucked a few minutes ago into pieces, Mary returned, followed shortly by Thor and Zelda. "Anybody know where Nils got to?" Mary asked conversationally.

"He's comin'," Thor replied. "He was down to the horse barn."

And, Sam thought, what a difference a generation made. Her father would have said, *He vas down to da horse house.* She didn't know what her mother would have said, she being long dead and buried back in Kansas City, Missouri. Apparently, her mother and father had been married just long enough to say "I do" and produce her. Her mother had died in childbirth, and shortly thereafter, her father, Sven, had found himself a more suitable bride. At least, one who didn't mind naming her kids after Norse-country gods and goddesses.

Sam had gotten her hands on the family Bible once, and had done her calculations. Her parents had been wed for only six months before her birth, and her mother, whose maiden name was listed as "Druzie Faye Geode," must have been a whore, by the sound of it. So when it came right down to brass tacks, she couldn't even be certain that Sven was her father.

She had never let it cripple their relationship, though. She just went on as if she'd never found out, and if Sven had a clue to her snooping, he'd never let on. He'd never treated her any differently than the others either, bless his heart. Of course, he had to have a good heart if he'd take some Kansas City hooker's word about "his" child.

But Sven had taken responsibility and married her anyway. Another good thing in his favor. So if Thor thought he was going to get into the whipping kind of trouble over this, he was sadly mistaken. Samantha knew their father better than that, and Thor's mother was no longer around to care. The West was hard on women, and she'd died from a snakebite one summer's day about four years ago. God bless her, Samantha thought. She'd never been anything but kind and caring, and although she'd been a stepparent to Samantha, Samantha had been raised to call her Mama.

The grease was starting to bubble in the frying pan, and she had most of the chicken pieces battered and floured. Mr. Walker loved her chicken, all right. He demanded it at least six times a week. She stepped back from the stove top just in case, and slid the first pieces into the grease, adding the rest a piece at a time until she was out of pieces to add.

"There," she said, crossing her arms. "Two hens ought to hold him for a while." She tipped her head. "At least a half hour or so . . ." She went back to her post at the window, although this time not to stare at Thor and Zelda, who were hard at work in the kitchen, mashing potatoes while Mary snapped the beans and Nils polished his boots for the third time. Instead, it was to watch for Slocum.

The three men rode down into Tucson.

They had lost sight of the rustlers long ago, but Slocum trailed them into town as far as he could before their tracks became obscured in the muddle of others. Once he was certain they'd lost the trail, he said, "Well, boys, I say we go get us a drink. They're more likely to turn up at a saloon than in the middle of a street."

Goose nodded agreeably. Xander still had the same smile on his face as he'd had when they'd had the conversation about his true parentage.

To tell the truth, Slocum didn't know exactly how to feel about that.

Still, that didn't keep him from reining in Speck out front of the Palace Bar in Tucson, and slipping down to earth. The other two followed his lead, all three tying their horses at the rail and sauntering through the saloon's batwing doors.

There was a crowd inside despite it being only midafternoon. Men lined the bar, painted women were gamboling at the bar and on men's laps, and most all the tables were filled with poker games in progress. Slocum muscled his way up to the bar, creating an opening for Goose and Xander, and ordered a whiskey. The whole time, he was scanning the crowd for signs to tell him that somebody had spent the night in the open.

"Hey there!" said a voice from behind him. He turned toward it and found it had come from a grinning cowpoke with dark hair. And a good bit of dried mud splashed up over his pants legs.

Immediately, Slocum was on the alert. "Hey, yourself," he replied.

The cowpoke looked him up and down, taking in Goose and Xander, too. "Seems you fellas got caught out in that goose-drownder we had last night."

Slocum forced a friendly smile. "Looks like it got you, too." He nodded down toward the hand's legs and boots.

"Yessiree, it sure did. The night was clear as a mountain spring, then all of a sudden, BOOM! Felt like we'd got caught up on my ma's old washboard with her scrubbing at Pa's dungarees full tilt."

Slocum laughed, still casual. He said, "How come you found yourself out in the open last night? We're travelin' down to Bisbee." He waved his hand at Goose and the boy. "Should'a took the train."

Goose and Xander had stopped talking, and were paying attention to Slocum's conversation now. In particular, they were paying attention to the man he was conversing with.

The hand laughed. "Yeah, you should'a, all right. Hey, Chip!" he shouted across the room. A blond kid at one of the poker tables looked up. "These fellas got caught in that turd floater last night, too!"

"Sorry," Slocum said, holding his hand out. "My name's Slocum. This here's Xander, and that's Goose."

"Pleased to meetcha," said the hand, who couldn't have been over eighteen himself. He took Slocum's offered hand and shook it. "I'm Roy, and my pal over there, that's Chip."

Goose and Xander didn't offer their hands, but both nodded. Goose muttered, "Nice to meetcha."

Roy seemed to be puzzling something over in his mind. "Slocum," he finally said. "I heard that name before somewhere. You famous or anything?"

Slocum had his mouth halfway open when Xander cut in.

"You kiddin' me?" he said, looking shocked. "He's famous! They write books about him all the time!"

"I'll be damned," said Roy.

"They may write the damned books, but they sure don't do no research for 'em," Slocum groused. He turned to the bartender. "Can I get another whiskey down here?" He glanced at Goose's and Xander's glasses. "Make that two whiskeys and a beer." There he went again, playing papa, taking care of everybody.

He turned back to Roy. "Somebody told me about one that took place in the 'rugged mountains of Kansas.' Now, you know that the writer was never west of the Hudson River in his life, don't you?"

Roy laughed giddily, thinking he'd run across a real celebrity, and flagged down his friend, Chip, once again. "Hey, buddy!" he called. "Come meet a real famous man!"

Chip, who didn't look much older than Roy, looked up from his cards, then folded. He must not have had anything to speak of, Slocum thought. Weaving his way through the crowd, Chip came over to the bar.

"Somebody famous?" he asked once he reached them. He wasn't very tall, and Slocum had to tilt his head down to see his face. "Who?"

"You mean you ain't never heard of that Slocum feller they write them books about?" Roy asked, confident that he was one jump ahead of the game.

But Chip immediately lit up and looked Slocum square in the eye. "Holy cow!" was all he said, and then he pulled the hat off his head. "I just finished up another one'a those books, Mr. Slocum! I can't believe I'm meetin' you for real and true!" Then he grabbed Slocum's hand and pumped it like there was no tomorrow.

Slocum was getting to feel sort of bad, seeing as how he planned to march these boys down to the sheriff's office, but he overcame it. After all, he was certain they were the ones he'd been looking for.

"You boys live around here?" Xander said, trying to help.

Chip nodded. And Roy said, "We work for Mr. Smollets. He owns the Circle Cross, up north a ways."

Slocum nodded. "Runs cattle, does he?"

"Finest kind," said Chip. "Mostly Hereford crosses, and some straight range stock. As long as it's a cow, he'll run it, will Mr. Smollets." Behind him, Roy gave a snort.

"He's from England," Chip added, as if that would explain everything.

Slocum nodded and smiled, as if he understood completely. Then he held up one finger, saying, "Just a second there, fellas." He turned to Xander, and in the lowest of tones, told him to run and fetch the sheriff fast.

Then, as Xander exited the bar, he turned back around toward Chip and Roy. He was beginning to run out of anything civil to say to them, but Goose took up the slack, quizzing them on ranching in southern Arizona and asking if they had much fuss down here over water rights.

"Not as much as you might think," said Chip. "'Course now that the river here has gone all the way underground and the swamplands are gone, it's anybody's guess what'll happen next."

"Swamplands?" Goose asked, genuinely intrigued. "You got swamps around here?"

"Not so's I can remember, but when my daddy and mama came out, the whole west side of Tucson was a swamp with disease-carryin' bugs and great big fish. Heard an older feller say as how he'd caught a hundred-pounder in it."

"Catfish?" Goose asked.

Chip shrugged. "Don't rightly remember. Just the hundred-pound part is all I recall. We used to have plenty of game right near town, too. Critters used to come from all over to water at the swamp."

Slocum took another sip of his whiskey. "Fascinatin', boys. I remember those swamps, too. Long time ago. And hundred-pound fish weren't as uncommon as you might figure. I guess now the whole river system has gone underground?"

Roy nodded. "Yessir. 'Cept for every once in a while durin' the rainy season, it'll pop up here or there for a few days."

Behind Slocum, Goose said, "Here comes Xander."

Slocum glanced up, beyond Roy and Chip. Xander was indeed coming through the batwing doors, and the sheriff was right behind him, grinning like it was Christmas. These boys must have been sneak-thieving cattle for quite a while.

In truth, they had. When the sheriff slipped the cuffs on Chip—and knocked Roy to the ground in the process—both boys seemed genuinely shocked.

Roy's hand went immediately to his gun, but so did Slocum's. "Wouldn't do that if I were you," he said.

"Dang it anyhow!" Chip muttered. "I just can't catch a break!"

"Mayhap you just caught one, son," said Slocum, kindly as he followed the sheriff, Roy, and Chip from the bar, followed by Xander and Goose.

14

After Slocum filled out a rash of papers at the sheriff's office—and he and Goose and Xander all signed them—he said, "All right. Wanna go back to the bar and spend the night, or go back up to Hiram's place?"

Xander looked at Goose, and after a moment, Goose asked Slocum, "That offer to help me find them killers still good?"

Slocum grinned. "Good as gold."

"Then let's go on back to Mr. Walker's place," Goose said.

"We still gotta find Hiram's other cows that they took," Xander reminded them.

The sheriff spoke up. "Don't worry about that, boy. Me and my deputies'll ride on out there in the morning and see that all the cattle are collected. Reckon you can tell Hiram he can come over the day after and collect his beeves."

Slocum nodded. "Right nice of you."

The sheriff grunted, as if it were no trouble. Slocum

hoped he had a whole passel of deputies, because he hadn't seen hide nor hair of any more of Hiram's stock all the way in.

They hiked back down to the saloon and retrieved their horses, which they'd tethered beside a water trough, and set out.

"But we're goin' the wrong way!" said a worried-looking Xander.

"Don't be frettin' . . . son," said Goose around the lump in his throat. "Slocum's just takin' us the front way in."

And Slocum did.

They rode into the Walking W just as the sun was beginning to set. "Just in time for dinner!" Slocum said. He didn't add, *And a little after-dinner entertainment . . .*

Bodie Crane was hanging around near the main corral when they rode up, and at the news that everything was tidy with the sheriff, he offered to put up their horses for the night. Normally unwilling to let anybody but himself mess with his horse, Slocum felt his stomach growling so intensely that he tossed Bodie his reins and nodded his thanks. The others must have been as hungry as he was, because they almost raced him to the front door.

"All taken care of," Slocum said to Hiram, and then told him what had transpired. "The sheriff said you can ride out to the Smollets place the day after tomorrow and pick up the rest of your stock."

"Praise the Lord!" Hiram shouted, his hands clasped and eyes raised skyward. "Anything you want, just name it!"

"Just my pay," Slocum said. "And some dinner. We're about half starved!"

"Well, come in, come in the house! Samantha and her

crew just about have dinner on the table!" Hiram ushered them in posthaste. "Would you like to clean up?"

"No," said Xander.

Slocum looked at the kid. "Yes, we would," he said, and Xander nodded in reluctant agreement.

They went to their rooms and washed their hands and faces, and Slocum changed his shirt. The one he'd been wearing wasn't fit for mixed company, let alone just Hiram. He ran a rag over his dusty and mud-spattered boots, too, and slapped the hell out of his lower pants legs, raising quite a cloud of leftover desert in the process.

When they were gathered in the dining room, neither Goose nor Xander looked that much different, except for the clean hands. Xander had washed his face, too, and Goose had slicked down his hair with water and a comb, but all in all, they looked just about the same.

Hiram was the happiest of hosts, even more than usual. He chattered gleefully throughout the meal, which consisted of a prime rib roast, new potatoes, fresh corn and tomato salad, string beans, and deep-fried biscuits. This was followed by heaping portions of the best strawberry shortcake that Slocum had ever eaten, and he told Hiram as much.

"You keep on feeding us this good, you may have us for guests until fall, when your Betsy gets back!" Slocum said, just before he wiped his mouth with his napkin.

Hiram gushed, "Oh, you're welcome to stay till then and beyond, Slocum! All three of you! You got my cows back, and you can't imagine how much that means to me. It's hard to raise a crop of beef without any cows to bear 'em! That sonofabitch Smollets got nearly my whole crop of heifers for the year. Plus a steer or three."

Goose attempted to join the conversation, now that he was finally finished stuffing his mouth. "Oh, hell, Hiram, 'tweren't nothin'."

Xander said, "Well, it wasn't exactly *nothin'*. I 'bout ru-int my britches in that storm last night."

Hiram, having ordered after-dinner brandies all around, ignored Xander's britches difficulties and said, "I'm serious, boys. Stay as long as you like."

Slocum pursed his lips, then said, "That'd be up to Goose there. He's got some fellers that need trackin' down, and I aim to help him. Xander, too."

Hiram leaned forward. "Do I take it that these are the men who killed your brother and his son, Goose? The ones we were sending all those wires about?"

"That'd be them. Or just one man, more likely," Goose said. "They'll be sorry they ever messed with the Martin family."

Xander's brows shot up. "I'm a Martin?"

Goose, who had apparently forgotten to mention his last name, laughed and said, "Yup, you are."

"I thought he was a Slocum," Hiram said, head cocked to the side.

"Hiram, it's a real long story and I'd be happy to tell you all of it," Slocum said, "but in the morning. Frankly, about all I'm good for right at the moment is to have a good lie-down."

"Of course, of course!" said Hiram. "Ain't no rush at all! Finish your brandies, my friends, and then my home is yours. Sleep in as late as you'd like come morning. Hell, come the afternoon!"

Slocum waited until the house had settled down for the night before proceeding downstairs and back to the kitchen.

He hoped the kitchen staff was still working—or at least that Sam was, because he didn't want to go tippy-toeing around in the dark, trying to find her room.

But she was still up. And so were Nils and Mary. For all he knew, Zelda and Thor might come in at any second. And so he just said, "Howdy, everybody," walked over to the table, and sat down.

Mary was washing dishes, Nils was drying, and Sam was going over some sort of ledger. She looked up and smiled. "I wondered when you'd come back to see me, Slocum. Did you take care of Mr. Walker's rustler problem?"

He nodded. "That we did, ma'am. Day after tomorrow, Hiram can go pick up his cows at the Cross Circle. Or the Circle Cross. Forget which. But anyway, the sheriff and his deputies say they'll have the stock rounded up and ready by then."

"And what did Hiram agree to pay you?"

Slocum was taken a bit aback by the question. It wasn't really any of her business, just something between him and Hiram, and he told her so.

Smiling, she laughed a little and shook her head. "Don't take on," she said. "I'm the Walking W's manager, too. I write the checks."

"The checks?" Slocum didn't have much faith in paper money, whether it was written out by hand or printed by the U.S. government. He preferred cash money, preferably gold coin.

Samantha smiled again. "Oh, don't worry. Hiram already told me you prefer cash, and I have your envelope here somewhere . . ."

She riffled through the unused back pages of the ledger until she came to a sealed envelope. Written on the front, in

Hiram's scratchy scrawl, was "Slocum." Sam handed him the envelope, saying, "I know it's not polite, but please count it in front of me so we both know it's right." She paused a moment, then leaned toward him and whispered, "You know what a scatterbrain Hiram is."

She and Slocum shared a smile that started a warm tingle going in Slocum's nether regions, and he took a quick peek at Mary and Nils to make sure they hadn't noticed. They hadn't. When he turned back toward Sam, she was holding the envelope out toward him.

He took it, then slid his thumb under the flap, opening it. It felt heavy enough to make Slocum pretty sure that the whole five hundred dollars was in there, and when he counted it, it was—all in double eagles minted in San Francisco.

He allowed himself a small smile.

"All there?" asked Sam.

"It surely is," he replied, closing the envelope and licking the loose flap, sealing it. "Hiram always keeps his word." He shoved the bulging envelope into his vest pocket, then buttoned it. This was one envelope he didn't want to lose.

"Always means to keep it, you mean," Sam said, smiling.

Slocum smiled, and snorted out a laugh. "Yeah. He's got a good heart, all right."

"And deep pockets," Sam added.

Slocum chuckled. He wanted to lift her skirts right then and there and do her on the kitchen table. God, she was gorgeous!

She turned the pages of the ledger book back to the place where she'd been when he walked in, dipped her pen in the inkwell, and made a notation. Her handwriting was neat and precise, the letters slightly rounded and tilting. She was right-handed.

He didn't know why he found himself paying so much attention to the mundane when he should be escorting her to a quiet corner somewhere and getting on with it. But he found himself fascinated with everything she did, every little movement she made.

15

The second that Nils and Mary finished the dishes and said their good-nights, Samantha was on Slocum like white is on rice. She practically jumped him, straddling his lap and murmuring, "Sorry, sorry, they wouldn't go away, I've been waiting so long . . ." between passionate kisses.

Slocum didn't say or do a blessed thing besides kiss her back and gratefully hold her tight, searching for her dress's buttons and trying his damnedest not to explode in his pants.

She was an expert kisser, and in the time it took him to unbutton her bodice, her eager tongue had explored every corner of his mouth, every nook and cranny. And then her hands were on his chest, unbuttoning his shirt, even as he slipped the blouse from her shoulders, then the camisole, exposing round, full, gorgeous breasts, tipped with the color of the inside of a sea shell.

She didn't take his shirt off, just unbuttoned it all the way and slid her hands beneath it, her arms encompassing him as they kissed and kissed and kissed, her breasts pressing against his bare chest, her tight, swollen nipples softly scraping him, arousing him even more.

He was about to burst from his britches when her fingers at last released him, and he sprang up, fully erect. He was trying to decide whether to try to make it to her room or just take her right there when her fingers moved again, this time to her waist. A few simple motions later, and her skirt, then her slip, simply fell away.

She was wearing no undergarments.

"They're wraparound," she whispered into his ear jut before she nibbled on his earlobe, just before she lifted herself up, moved closer to him, and sat down, letting his cock impale her like a flagpole.

He let out an enormous grunt—of relief, of satisfaction, of need and gratitude and excitement and pure joy—as she began to move up and down, slowly at first, then with increasing rapidity. He slipped a hand between them to cup one breast, to play with its nipple, to fondle its soft weight. The other arm he kept around her, helping her hold her back straight as she pumped up and down, up and down.

She was moving more creatively now, sometimes with a side-to-side swirling motion that drove him crazy with ecstasy, and he knew she was ready to come—as was he. He waited until he felt the moment was just right, and then he pushed up into her, hard, as she came down on him.

As a result, he felt waves of an enormous orgasm overtake him, washing him clean, as she called out his name. In fact, she called it out several times before he had the presence of mind—and the motor skills—to cover her mouth.

As tired as he was, as tired to the bone, Xander had a hard time getting to sleep. The fact that his father was someone

different than the man he'd been led to believe was his father had shocked him, and Slocum's deft handling of the
apprehension of the cattle rustlers had impressed him. Also,
that Slocum was going to split the reward money, the
money the sheriff would be mailing him in a couple of
weeks, was a boon too good to be true!

He tossed and turned, thinking nonstop about the day's
events. It was just too much! He liked Goose—whom he
now had to call his pa, whether he believed it or not— and
Slocum was convinced of the misunderstanding. It must be
true. And he sure had Goose's coloring. He didn't understand how the dates worked exactly, but was too embarrassed to admit it. He supposed somebody would explain it
to him later.

He yawned again, and his head rolled sideways on the
pillow. He supposed that to have a father like Slocum, even
if it was only for a week, was something of an honor,
wasn't it? And Goose was no slouch himself compared to
Slocum. The two of them were cut from the same cloth.
Both were tall and rugged, and both knew their way around
horses and cattle—and rustlers!

Xander had never had such adventures in his life. And
finally, despite the way his mind whirled from subject to
subject, he fell asleep at about eleven o'clock.

Goose, too, had a hard time falling asleep. He was proud to
have found Xander, proud to have a son, but how was he
going to explain him once he got back home? Molly and
the girls would certainly be shocked to find out that their
husband and daddy had ever had sexual congress with anyone but their mama. He loved Mariska. She was as soft
and fair as a spring day, with hair the same color as his—
although not so gray, he thought, his mouth quirking up—

and the girls were all the same. The oldest and youngest were redheads, the way he had once been and Xander was now, and the middle girl, Annie, was a strawberry blonde.

Mariska had come over from Russia on her father's ship when he came to trade for pelts, and the first time Goose saw her, he knew, he just knew. Exactly two weeks after the day they met, they were married. He shook his head. Hell, they couldn't even speak each other's languages! But Bill Maguire, who ran the Hudson Trading Company, spoke some Russian, and he'd been a big help. He'd even helped Goose propose!

He remembered standing in the church, Mariska at his side, and Bill translating, with his brother standing on the other side as his best man, while they said their vows. What a day that had been!

And now, he found he had a son, a son almost fully grown, a son who was, well, quite a man. Well, he had a lot to do before he had to tell Mariska and the girls. For now, he was just going to take things as they came. And the first thing that came to him was sleep.

Samantha led a happy and sated Slocum back to her room, which turned out to be quite spacious. While Slocum had expected little more than a closet with a rough bed shoved into the corner, she had a roomy bedroom, a small sitting room lined with bookshelves and pictures, and off to the side, a small washroom. It was here that she directed him first, and he washed up in the basin and combed his hair in the mirror. She even had a shuttered outhouse tucked into one corner, and he happily took advantage of that, too.

In the opposite corner was some kind of contraption that he couldn't figure out, but when he asked Sam, she said it was a "shower bath." When Slocum screwed up his face, she just smiled and went to the pump. There, she flipped a little switch near the valve, then said, "Take off your clothes and I'll demonstrate."

Curious, Slocum stripped and so did she—and she had a beaut of a body— and then she pulled him up to stand on the wooden grate that was the floor of the shower bath. She smiled up at him, although the two of them barely fit once she'd pulled the curtain closed around it. She glanced over at a second pump handle, near the wall, but a pump handle with no spigot. It just kind of stuck out of the wall. She said, "Now, pump."

"What?"

"Pump. You'll see."

Shrugging, Slocum grabbed the handle with one arm and began to pump it up and down. Nothing happened, but she encouraged him by saying, "Keep going, Slocum."

He did, and less than a minute later, it began to rain! In the house!

He was shocked, and he stopped pumping.

The rain stopped, too.

He looked up to see some kind of round metal thing sticking down from the ceiling, something that slowly dripped water. It was flattened on the bottom, sort of like an upside-down funnel, with the small end poking up into the ceiling, and the wide end covered with more metal that was pierced with at least a hundred little holes.

"What the hell?" he grumbled.

"Come on," she urged, "pump it again! It'll keep going for about two minutes without touching it, once you get it really going!"

Instantly, he got it! The pump handle was for a longer spigot that ended overhead, forcing water down through the pipe and the little holes—a shower bath!

He started pumping with gusto, and in no time they were flooded with lukewarm water from the underground well. The water coming down from overhead—and not being cold, like a waterfall—was quite a sensation, and Slocum admired it. He immediately decided that if he ever settled down and found a place with enough ground water, he was going to put one of these things in his house, too.

Sam soaped his chest and arms, and then got a little more "personal" with her scrubbing. She ran the bar of slippery soap and her sudsy hands along—and into—every nook and cranny of his body, arousing him almost incidentally. But arousing him nonetheless.

And he returned the favor, borrowing the soap when she was finished and lathering her all over, lingering at her full breasts as long as possible. running the soap leisurely between her legs and over the patch of short hair that covered it, until, whimpering, she dug her nails into his shoulders. He moved down to bathe her legs and feet, and heard her pumping more water as he went.

At last, they were both rinsed clean and free of the last of the soap, and they let the shower slowly stop. They stood there, hugging and kissing, surrounded by the still-closed shower curtain and the memory of the luxurious flowing water, until Sam said softly, "Come along, Slocum. I want you inside me so bad that I'm about to burst!"

Eagerly, he followed her out into the bedroom—never thinking to grab his clothes—and still sopping wet, he pulled her down with him on the wide, soft bed. As her breasts made contact with his chest with soft, slippery *plops,* she rolled to the side, pulling him atop her.

He gladly went. He was still kissing her, although his lips had moved from her mouth to her ears, from her throat to her breast, where he laved a tight, upstanding nipple with his tongue, then slowly traced the line of the crease on the underside of the breast.

"Slocum, hurry," she whispered, and he moved between her legs. Immediately, her knees rose to grip his hips. He was already as hard as a rock, and he centered himself over her core, then suddenly, forcefully plunged in.

She didn't sigh with it, but instead took in enough air to fill her lungs, her chest belling upward with the effort and her hands digging into his muscular shoulders.

He began to thrust into her, faster and faster, twisting slightly every now and then with her rising to meet him, stroke for stroke, until she began to come. Which didn't take very long. When he felt her rising, he sped up his movements and clamped his lips on her nipple, sucking as hard as he could while he flicked the pebblelike tip with his tongue.

She came—massively, hugely, immensely—sending him over the crest, too, and, he thought, nearly bucking him to the ceiling in her enthusiasm.

"Whoa, gal," he whispered as he moved to her mouth, kissing the corners as she panted. Tears were running down her cheeks. He brushed them away with his thumbs. "It's all right, Sam. You're home, in your bed, with me."

Suddenly, her arms moved to encompass his shoulders, to ring him lovingly. "I know, Slocum," she said. "I know."

16

The next morning dawmed bright and clear, but Slocum, Goose, and Xander weren't up to see it. Samantha got up when her alarm went off at four thirty as usual, then reset it for nine thirty for the still-sleeping Slocum. Goose finally wandered downstairs at about nine, and Xander didn't make it until ten.

Goose and Slocum, still gratefully rubbing the sleep from his eyes, waited till Xander came down before they heeded Hiram's advice to get on out to the dining room and get themselves some grub. Slocum had cheated a little— Sam had shoved some fried ham at him when he went through the kitchen, and then some fried potatoes. He did not mention this to Goose, who looked to be starving to death, but who was bound and determined to wait for his son.

When Xander finally came down, Goose rushed him into the dining room, and they all sat down to a huge breakfast that included more of the fried ham, plus hash browns, applesauce, corn bread, and cactus jelly. Hiram, who had already eaten breakfast, joined them for corn bread and cactus jelly and three big cups of coffee.

It seemed he was a bottomless pit.

After breakfast, Slocum and the others walked down to see to their horses. Slocum gave Speck a good brushing from head to tail to hoof, cleaned out his hooves and grained him, then led him out to an empty paddock and let him loose.

"Looks like he's enjoyin' himself," said Xander, who was leading Eagle out. Speck, at that moment, was rolling vigorously in the dirt, undoing most of Slocum's grooming, but Slocum didn't mind. He'd brush him down again later in the afternoon. And after all, a horse was a horse was a horse.

Grinning, he shook his head.

"Wish I could teach him to groom himself," he said.

Xander grinned back. "Looks like he is." He opened the gate and moved Eagle into the paddock, then unsnapped his lead. The horse immediately ducked his head and bucked out in the rear, and began to tear around the enclosure. "Fulla piss an' vinegar, ain't he?" Xander asked.

As Speck climbed to his feet, shook himself off in a mighty cloud of dust, and then took off after Eagle, Slocum said, "He ain't the only one."

Both he and Xander laughed as the horses gamboled freely in the corral.

Kip came out of the barn last, leading Goose, and although Slocum figured it was in the wrong order, he just smiled. "Anxious?"

Goose nodded. "Been like this since the second he heard them other two out here." As they skidded up to the corral gate, Goose mopped his brow. "He's a whole different critter under saddle." He turned Kip in with the other two, and Kip immediately joined in the game.

The three fellows hung over the fence for some time, watching the horses blow off steam, before Goose checked his pocket watch. "Lunchtime!" he announced.

"Already?" asked Slocum. Goose must've had a clock in his stomach.

Xander craned his head to look at Goose's watch and grinned. "He's right. It's twelve on the dot."

"Wonder what we're havin' for lunch," Goose said as he backed away from the fence and turned toward the house.

"I don't care," said Slocum, and when Xander hiked a brow, he added, "Whatever it is, it's bound to be great."

"I'll second that," said Xander.

"And I'll third it," Goose said. He was already ten feet away from them and making for the house.

After a wonderful midday meal, Slocum left the others in the house to wander down to the corral again. The horses were dozing in the midday heat, although they were standing head-to-tail under the shadow of the barn's roof overhang.

Slocum shook his head. It seemed like his wasn't the only horse who'd taken advantage of the paddock's gravelly floor to get himself a good back scratch. Both Eagle and Kip were covered with a film of dust, too.

As Slocum leaned on the top rail, watching them swish their tails, Apollo wandered up from one of the other barns. "Hear you put a stop to the rustlin'," he said.

Slocum nodded. "So they tell me. I'm waitin' to see just how many more of those missing head the sheriff can come up with."

"Tomorrow?"

"Yup."

"We're gonna have to start early," said Apollo. "It's a long haul over to the Circle Cross. Or the Cross Circle. Or whatever Smollets calls it."

"You don't sound as if you've got too much time for him."

Apollo nodded. "You could say that. At least, you put him outta business forever. He'll likely spend the rest of his days over in Yuma Prison. Serves him right, too, if anybody was to ask me."

Slocum dug into a pocket and pulled out the last of his ready-mades. He lit one, and said, "Reckon Hiram would agree with you there. Reckon a lot of folks around these parts would."

Apollo nodded. "A lot of folks are bound to say that Yuma's too good for him. Hangin' would be more fittin'. See, this rustlin' business has been goin' on for years. A little stock here, a little stock there. This is the first time Hiram's been hit, though." He leaned his elbows on the fence.

"Too far from Smollets' place?" Slocum exhaled a cloud of smoke.

"I reckon. My guess is that they just come across that little box canyon you found and decided it'd make a perfect holdin' pen. Hell, even the boss didn't know it was there," Apollo added, tipping his head up toward the house.

Slocum's brow furrowed. "He didn't?"

"Nope. He's got a pretty big spread here, and you can't investigate every nook and cranny when you've gotta be home for every meal." He smiled. "Sorry. That ain't kind. But Mrs. Walker used to insist he be there for every feeding or else. You'd think she was fattening him up for market."

Slocum laughed. "Seems like he can do that on his own

these days." He ground his smoke out underfoot. "Guess I'd best get back on up to the house."

"Yeah, Mr. Walker'll be lookin' for somebody to share his afternoon brandy with," Apollo said with a kindly smile. "Wish he'd ask me!" He laughed. "Well, good seein' you. We'll meet again tomorrow when we go to pick up the beeves, won't we?"

"Reckon so," said Slocum.

Apollo walked off the way he'd come, and Slocum headed on up to the house, leaving the horses to a well-deserved doze.

Slocum didn't spend any time with Hiram. He peeked into the study, and finding it empty, grinned and headed for the dining room en route to the kitchen. Inside, he found Samantha, sitting alone at the big kitchen table and reading a catalogue.

She looked up and immediately broke out in a smile. "Good afternoon," she said, and motioned to the chair next to her.

Slocum pulled it out and sat down. First, he lifted her hand and kissed the palm. "How are you doing today, you little butterfly?"

She almost giggled. "Butterfly? I've never been called that before." Then she took his hand and kissed his knuckles. "In answer to your question, I'm fine. In fact, I'm delightful, splendid, and fit as a fiddle. You do a lot for a girl, Mr. Slocum. And by the way, I've been meaning to ask. Do you have a first name, too?"

"John," he answered without thinking. He normally didn't give his first name, even if he was asked, but this girl was special.

"John," she repeated. It didn't sound common when uttered through her lips. She added, "I like that. It's a good, strong name."

"Thanks," he said, "but that's just between you and me, Sam, all right?"

She nodded, smiling. She set aside the catalogue and took his hand in both of hers. "You're wonderful," she said softly. "You're wonderful, and I wish you could stay here forever, but I know you'll be moving on soon."

He quirked a brow. "How do you know that?"

She smiled. "Experience. You're the travelin' sort. And you can't change that. It's just the way you're made."

Slocum looked down. "True." How had she recognized that without being told? Actually, he was glad that she had. By the time he got ready to settle down, she'd probably be a grandmother.

He said, "I ain't beggin'—well, I guess I am—but I'l like at least one more night with you. I ain't never known anybody like you."

She said, "Thanks, I think. And I don't intend to let you ride out without another night in my bed, John. Sorry, Slocum."

He said, "S'all right. Tomorrow we're all gonna ride over to—"

"Smollets' place. I know. Hiram already told me to pack up lunch and dinner. Breakfast, too, if I know him."

Slocum nodded. "Apollo said it's a fair piece."

"So you'll need your sleep tonight. Let's plan on the day after tomorrow, all right? There's going to be a wedding the day after—Thor and Zelda—when the circuit rider comes through, and I think Hiram would really like you to be here for it."

Slocum smiled. "Tell the groom congratulations for me."

Just then, the door to the back hall swung in and Thor

entered. Slocum and Samantha quickly let go of each other's hands, and Slocum said, "I hear you're gettin' hitched. Congratulations!"

Thor said, "Thank you, Mr. Slocum, but I don't know. Sam, Zelda's upstairs makin' a fuss 'cause she doesn't think her wedding dress fits right. Mary's tryin' to help her, but I think she's just making it worse. Could you maybe—"

Sam stood up, "I'm on it like a duck on a june bug, Thor," she said, and marched toward the door, pausing only to say, "See you later, Slocum."

The way she said it gave him an erection all over again, and he had to sit at the table and make small talk with Thor for quite a while before he could get up.

Over on the Smollets spread, Sheriff Black and four of his deputies were rounding up cattle. Over two thousand head so far. Black had taken Smollets into custody already and sent him back to the jail with two deputies. Smollets's other hands were corralled, too, along with a kid named Milo Herrick. From what Black had been able to tell so far, he figured the kid, at least, would get off easy—he hadn't taken part in any of the thefts, and all he'd done was to drive out to the box canyon each day and feed and water stock.

Black knew the judge. He also figured that he'd let the kid skate on time served, or maybe just a few weeks in the city jail.

But it would be different for Smollets and the rest.

One of his deputies came galloping up, and Sheriff Black stopped his mare. "What is it, Hollings?" he called.

The deputy shouted back, "Found another box canyon. You ain't gonna believe it, Jasper!"

Black shouted, "Believe what?"

The deputy, Rance Hollings, reined his lathered horse to a halt next to Black's. "We found another box canyon," he repeated. The countryside was riddled with them, it appeared. Black himself had never been out this way, had never had a reason to come out, and the area was a mystery to most of his deputies, too.

"You found another box canyon," Black said. "So?"

"It's big," said Rance.

"So?"

"And there's about another thousand head in it—Circle W, Walking W, Jagged M, Trace D, you name it."

It took a moment for the sheriff to register this, but when he did, he said, "Holy shit!" under his breath, then shouted, "Hector! Follow Rance!"

Hector, another of Black's deputies, who was hired for the day, nodded his head, then took out after Rance, who was already galloping back up north.

This was one very big screwed-up mess, Black was thinking. He'd seen brands that had been altered years ago and brands that looked to have been altered only last week. Mostly on cows with calves at their sides, some on young heifers. Smollets had been smart, all right: smart to steal just a few head at a time, and smart to steal mostly cows that he could breed for years to come, with no one the wiser as to their ancestry. If it hadn't been for Hiram Walker and his hired gun, Smollets might have gotten away with it for decades.

17

Hiram's "hired gun" had enjoyed one helluva breakfast, although he hadn't had the best night's sleep knowing Sam was right downstairs, cooking her heart out so that Hiram would have a great feast for today.

At the moment, Hiram and his men, plus Slocum, Goose, and Xander, were on their way to pick up Hiram's cattle. They had already come to the Smollets place, had lunch—and Slocum could not believe the bounty that Sam had supplied them with—and gotten on their way. The sheriff's tracks went toward the northeast, and they followed.

Hiram—with Apollo at his side—took the lead. Slocum was mighty glad that Apollo was up there. Hiram had never been much as a tracker, and it seemed that his years of wedded bliss had done nothing to improve things. Additionally, he had the worst seat on a horse that Slocum had ever seen. It had been bad before, but all the extra pounds Betsy, with Samantha's help, had managed to put on him had made him a sorry sight. With every step his horse took, Slocum could see the reverberations traveling through the fat all the way to his neck.

It wasn't pretty.

But at least he was giving it a try. Slocum had met a lot of fellows who'd simply sent out the hands, then retired with a bottle of bourbon.

Not that Hiram wasn't well stocked for this little jaunt. One of the packhorses—there were five carrying all sorts of comestibles—bore enough Who Hit John to stock a small bar, plus all the china and crystal to go with it.

About an hour from the ranch, they spotted a cloud of dust on the horizon. A cloud that pretty soon contained a few cattle, then a lot of cattle, and then an enormous amount of cattle! By the time Hiram's men and Sheriff Black's men met up, Slocum estimated that the herd was over three thousand strong, counting calves. "Well, I'll be goddamned," he muttered.

"You and me both," said Goose, beside him and wide-eyed.

Xander, who had never been on a roundup, let alone one like this, said, "Holy criminy! Did Mr. Smollets steal *all* these cows?"

"I imagine so," Slocum said, and nudged Speck up to where Hiram, Apollo, and the sheriff were talking.

Sheriff Black doffed his hat. "Afternoon, Slocum. Believe we got a few cattle for Hiram here, along with every other rancher in the valley."

"Yes, yes!" gushed Hiram. "Look at them, just look!" he said, waving his arms around. Then he hugged himself tight, as if he was trying to hold in all that excitement but was fighting an uphill battle.

Sheriff Black snorted out a laugh. Then he asked Slocum, "You got a horse that can cut?"

Slocum nodded. "Yeah. Why, you want to start sortin' 'em out here?"

"Don't see why not. Once you get yours outta the way, the rest'll be easier for us to handle."

Slocum rested both hands on the saddle horn, then leaned forward. "I can see where you've got a problem." Five men trying to move three thousand head of cattle? It was unheard of. Slocum said, "Sure. I'll need to talk to Hiram's men and figure out who's gonna do the ketch pen and such."

"Good enough," said the sheriff, and he signaled to his men to hold off on pushing the cattle.

They worked all afternoon and into the evening, and when the sun finally set, even the game Speck was worn out. But Slocum kept cutting out Hiram's stock as long as he could see the brands, along with Apollo, who had a pretty fine cutting horse himself. By the time the lack of light forced them to quit, they figured they had all but nine or ten head accounted for.

"Maybe," said Sheriff Black. He pulled up some ground next to Slocum, and handed him a plate heaped with food.

"Samantha strikes again," said Slocum, accepting it greedily.

"Yeah, she can really pay out a spread!" said Xander around the chicken leg.

Slocum noticed that everyone—including the sheriff's deputies—was dining from Hiram's stores, but Hiram seemed fine with that. He had long since set his plate aside, and was currently working his way into a bottle of Napoleon brandy. With the sheriff, Slocum noted. He also noted that Hiram had already spent more money on those cattle—counting the extra outlay of food, the cash he'd paid Slocum, and now this feast of a "picnic"—than they were worth. It seemed to Slocum that there were a bunch of other spreads that were going to come out of this deal a lot better than Hiram would.

But it wasn't his business. He dug into his food. Eating on fine china was something of a change, especially when you were seated Indian style and on your butt around a campfire. But Slocum thought to himself, grinning as he dug into his mashed potatoes and gravy, that it was something he could probably get used to.

A few moments later—and three bites of potatoes, six bites of cold fried chicken, and two bites of peas and carrots later as well—Slocum saw young Nils walk up out of the gloom. He'd been sent along to guard the food, so to speak, and make sure the dishes got cleaned.

He carried something before him like it was a precious object, and he made right for Slocum, stopping before him. "Just for you, sir," he said, whisking away the napkin cover. "Strawberry-rhubarb pie, with Miss Sam's regards."

As Slocum took the pastry and set the pan down carefully beside him, he was thinking, *What a girl, what a girl!*

The morning dawned bright and clear. After a quick breakfast—Sam's good vittles being pretty much used up—Slocum and Apollo quickly cut out their last few cows, and Hiram's men were the first bunch out, herding Hiram's cattle ahead of them.

About halfway back to the ranch, they ran into a curious bunch: a man perched in a one-rider shay that was covered with a colorful parasol and drawn by a fancy, high-stepping pony with a short-cropped tail. This sight was surrounded by outriders of the more standard variety. Hiram raised his hand and called out, "Cord! Cord, you old scalawag!" before he twisted toward Slocum and said, "C'mon. There's somebody you've gotta meet!"

Slocum followed him at a slow jog to the place where the funny little wagon had stopped, then watched as Hiram—with the help of a couple of Cord's outriders—dismounted. Hiram approached the shay, swinging his arms about and shouting, "By God, Cord, it's good to see you!" and when he reached it, he bent over and hugged the driver.

The driver looked a little embarrassed, but shook it off when Hiram suddenly turned and said, "Cord, this here's Slocum. Our rustler wrangler."

Slocum nodded. "Mr. Cord."

Cord gave him a toothy smile. "No, it's just Cord. My name's Cord Whipple, Mr. Slocum." He leaned toward the still-mounted Slocum and held out his hand.

Slocum slipped off his horse, took a few steps, and took Cord's hand. The man might have had bum legs, Slocum thought, but he had a firm handshake. "It's just Slocum, Cord. No mister to it 'less my daddy's around."

Cord Whipple laughed. "I got the sheriff's telegram last evening, Hiram, and we just set out. We're to meet him somewhere out here." His hand to his eyes, he scanned the horizon.

Slocum said, "He's not far back. We just left him a couple of hours ago. But he's got over a couple thousand more head to move than we do."

Cord looked shocked. "My God!"

Hiram nodded. "There's a mighty mess of 'em. And every single one thieved accordin' to the sheriff."

"Who did this thief Smollets steal from?" Cord demanded, muttering, "And I thought he was my friend!"

"Everybody," Slocum said. He walked back and mounted Speck. "Sheriff says it's been goin' on for years. Most of the ranchers didn't know they were gettin' hit, on account of he rustled so few at a time, and mostly took cows, not steers."

Cord shook his head. "I'll be bloody well damned . . ."

Just then, Slocum noticed a cloud of dust beginning to show on the eastern horizon. "Here comes Sheriff Black with the cattle." He pointed, and both Cord and Hiram looked and nodded.

Slocum tipped his hat to Cord. "You'll excuse me, but we'd best get our bunch movin' 'fore they take a notion to rejoin the big herd."

"Certainly, certainly, old man," Cord replied. "Honored to have made your acquaintance, Slocum. Honored!"

Smiling, Slocum tipped his hat, then wheeled Speck back around to the others. "Move 'em out!" he called.

Goose echoed the same order to Apollo, and Apollo echoed it to the men, and suddenly the whole mob came alive: the cattle moving and scrambling for position, and the men whistling and talking and whipping them forward.

Slocum left Hiram and Cord behind, and scrambled to catch up.

"Can you help me button this up?" Sam asked.

A grinning Slocum obliged, although reluctantly. "I'd druther help you take it off again," he said.

She laughed. "There're few things Hiram notices or even cares about, but dinner being late is surely at the top of the list."

Slocum said, "So I've noticed." He put the final button

into place, then opened the bedroom door for her. It had been her idea to make love—when Slocum rode in, he was dead-tired, or thought he was anyway—and she'd grabbed him by the collar and pulled him through the kitchen and into the back hall, pulling off his clothes as she went.

Frankly, he hadn't done much to resist.

Xander and Goose were somewhere around, although they didn't make themselves known, but when Slocum walked out of the dining room, he found Hiram in the study, almost drunk on the last of the Napoleon brandy.

Frankly, Slocum was astonished that it had lasted as long as it had.

"Mind if I join you?" Slocum asked, and when Hiram clutched a little harder at the neck of the brandy bottle, he added, "I'll take a whiskey, if you don't mind."

That was a different proposition entirely. At least, judging by Hiram's body language, it was. He immediately ushered Slocum into a chair and moved to the little portable bar to pour Slocum a drink.

Slocum started to stop him, but leaned back instead. He could take a liking to being waited on.

When Hiram returned, handing Slocum what must have been a triple, he sat in his own chair again and picked up where he'd left off on the brandy. Between sips and sniffs, he said, "You're gonna stay around for the aftermath, right?"

The only aftermath Slocum could think of was the trial, and he said, "Reckon not. Don't cotton to courtrooms much."

Hiram waved his hands. "No, no. I mean before that. The part with the grateful ranchers."

"Huh?"

Hiram didn't answer him. Instead, he just laughed. And

when Slocum screwed up his face, thinking that Hiram had either drunk himself into hysteria, or just plain gone crazy, Hiram finally said, "You just stick around a few days. You'll see, you'll see."

18

Harvey Smollets sat in his cell, slowly simmering. Slocum. That was the name of the "gentleman" who had found him out and who was responsible for his being incarcerated. Probably for the rest of his life, or so that moron of a sheriff had told him. And probably the same for his hands, who were currently occupying the jail's two other cells and complaining about the food.

Slocum. The name kept running through his head like a bad dream, one from which he couldn't wake up. He was still reeling from the sheriff's having shown up on his doorstep this morning and sending him and his remaining men to town—in handcuffs!—with two of the sheriff's deputies.

"I am a leading citizen!" he grumbled to himself. "I deserve better treatment than he would give a common thief!"

Harvey Smollets considered himself a thief, all right, but the most high-class sort. Not like some cheap pickpocket, not like some prowling cat burglar. He considered himself above those kinds. His trade was a stealthy one, if it was done right. Did these people know how many years he had invested in this backward territory!

Slocum.

Some hired gun, according to Roy and Chip, the two idiots who'd just had to get to town to have a drink and a woman, and had talked to Slocum. Who had figured it out.

The deputies who had brought Smollets and his men into town had ridden back out directly, and now they were in the hands of a charwoman, who was currently unlocking the door to the cells to collect the dinner plates. Thoughtfully, Smollets rubbed at his side. It had worked before. It would work again.

He waited, stretched out on his cot, until she had picked up the plates from the other cells. And when she came to his cell, demanding his plate, he sat up, clutching at his side, and attempted to hand it to her. But he dropped it halfway there, then tumbled off the cot to the floor, groaning.

The woman yelled at him a few times and kicked at the cell door, but he answered her with nothing more than dramatic groans and growls of pain, willing from her the key, willing her to use it.

"Oh, fiddlesticks!" he heard her grumble, and then he heard a more welcome sound—the key in his door. He stayed exactly where he was, twitching and groaning occasionally, doubled up in theatrical agony—how pleased he was that he'd spent those years on the stage in his youth! He'd still be there if his father's money hadn't given out right along with his father . . . and right along with the final closing curtain of *Miss Harrington's Veil*. He had played the third lead in a poorly staged production, but one had to start somewhere, didn't one?

Life was sometimes not fair, let alone lenient, as the plate collector was about to learn.

Still grumbling, she knelt beside him, saying, "Mister! Hey, mister! You need the doc?" He was amazed that she didn't reprimand him for the broken dishes. Well, perhaps she was about to, but he didn't give her a chance.

When she lowered her face—trying to get a look at his, he assumed—he sprang. It was the surprise of it that led to her demise. That, and the choke hold he immediately applied to her neck. It took less than a second before he heard her neck crack, and felt her then go limp.

She was dead.

That was easy, he thought, disentangling himself from her hefty form. When he was on his feet once more, he nudged her over with his toe. Why, she was an old woman! Fifty at the least. He barked out a laugh. What a fool Tucson's sheriff must be, to have entrusted five desperate cattle thieves to someone's grandmother!

Well, no longer.

He fiddled about until he found the keys, and unlocked the cells of the other four boys. "Is she . . . is she . . ." Milo kept repeating.

"She is dead, Milo," Smollets said, sounding like a schoolmaster. "And that's enough." He now addressed the entire contingent of those who had once been his ranch hands. "I suggest that you fellows split up when you ride out. And ride as far as you can." Symbolically, he brushed his hands over his vested front. "You are on your own. It has been a distinct pleasure working with you." The "distinct pleasure" part was pushing it a bit, but he'd only take this particular stage once.

And with that, he opened the cell block's door and exited the jail, leaving the hands behind to dumbly stare at one another.

It took them an hour to work up the intestinal fortitude to peep out the jail's front door, and by that time, Smollets had retrieved his gun and his horse and was headed not for home, not for the wide-open spaces, but for Hiram Walker's ranch.

To find Slocum.

Back at Hiram's ranch, the four men, including Xander, were just sitting down to another fabulous dinner. Roast beef au jus and scalloped potatoes were the centerpiece of at least ten or twelve dishes that Slocum counted, and as usual he made a hog of himself. Although he didn't feel alone—everybody else ate hearty, too, especially Hiram and Xander, who was, after all, a growing boy.

Again, servants lurked in the corners of the dining room, pouring coffee, bringing out further culinary surprises, and whisking away plates and replacing them deftly. Slocum found that once you got used to the servants, you didn't exactly notice them that much. Well, not at all really. They, and their services, just got to be part of the woodwork unless something caused one of them to speak. And being seen but not heard must have been Hiram's top priority. Except for the occasional "Good evening, sir," or "May I take your plate, sir?" the service was devoid of servants' chatter.

Of course, Hiram filled up the empty air, the old gasbag. He talked about his cattle, going on and on about how relieved, how completely and utterly and purely happy, he was to have them back on their home turf.

Slocum let most of Hiram's chatter wash over him. He figured it was about time for Apollo and his men to be coming home, after herding the cattle on farther to the rich grazing land that Hiram swore lay to the west. Plenty of good grama grass, he'd told Slocum earlier. It would explain why they'd seen so few head while they were out looking for rustlers, so Slocum had held his peace.

At any rate, he hoped that Sam had made enough extra to send leftovers to Apollo and his men down at the bunkhouse. If anybody deserved a meal fit for a king, it was those boys. They'd worked long and hard all day and into the evening, and had eaten a whole lot more trail dust than they'd signed on for.

By the time dessert came around, Slocum was full as a tick, but the lemon meringue pie perked him up. He ate two big pieces and loved every mouthful.

After all was said and done, and the dishes had been cleared away, he would have happily retired to bed—well, Sam's bed anyhow—had not Hiram insisted they all join him in the study for brandy and cigars.

Somebody had managed to dig up a new bottle of Napoleon, and while Hiram poured it, Slocum helped himself to a cigar. They were from Havana, and were the finest kind. If he used his imagination, he could almost pick up the fragrance of the sweat from the Cuban girl's thigh the cigar had been rolled on.

He gladly took his glass of brandy from Hiram, as did Goose and a puzzled Xander, and was slowly rolling the liquid about in his snifter when he saw Xander raising the glass to his lips.

He caught the boy's eye and signaled him not to drink, but to swirl his glass. He followed Slocum's directions, and a smile spread over his face as the aroma rose to his nose.

"Good, huh?" he asked Xander as Hiram struck a match and held it out to light Slocum's cigar. It wasn't a courtesy he was used to, but he took advantage of it anyway, puffing in the rich taste of Cuban-grown leaves. "By God, Hiram, that's quite a cigar," he said after rolling the smoke over his tongue.

"Thanks!" Hiram replied. He was holding a match to Goose's cigar at the moment. "I have 'em rolled special for me. Special blend and everything."

"You've got fine taste in tobacco," Slocum replied, adding, "just like everything else." Actually, Hiram's taste in food and drink echoed Slocum's—it was just that Hiram could afford to indulge his whims, whereas Slocum usually couldn't. He thought about Hiram's earlier offer, and decided to stay around for a few days.

It's only polite, he told himself, smiling.

"You ain't kiddin' about these cigars!" Goose piped up next to him. "Don't believe I ever tasted such fine tobacco! You sure you don't wanna try it?" he said to Xander, who had turned down the offer of a cigar.

"I'm sure," the boy said, "though thank you very much anyhow, Mr. Walker. It's just that I tried a cigarette one time, and I threw up. Hate to think what one of them big ol' cigars would do to me!"

Slocum and Hiram laughed, although Goose looked half embarrassed. "Good choice then," said Slocum, nodding. Xander nodded back and kept swirling and sniffing his brandy. He seemed content enough, and Slocum was pleased. Goose quickly resigned himself to having a non-smoker for a son, or anyway appeared to, and swirled his drink again before he took a sip.

He also appeared to enjoy that greatly, because a big smile spread over his face after he swallowed, and he said, "Mighty fine, mighty fine."

"So tell me, Slocum," Hiram said. "What the hell have

you been up to these past—what is it now?—two or three years?"

It was an awfully long list and Slocum didn't know where to begin. He told Hiram so. And he also told him that he'd rather hear about the cattle business down around Tucson—which he actually couldn't care less about.

But he'd touched on one of Hiram's favorite subjects, and Hiram grinned and started talking about free range-land and taxes and getting good hands and roundups. Talking about those things, Slocum decided, had to be Hiram's main gift next to eating.

19

At about nine, Smollets had settled into a comfy roost up above—and to the west of—Hiram's ranch house. He was waiting for the lights upstairs to go on, and for Slocum to pass by a window. He was ready for fast action, was Smollets. His horse was tethered down below, ready to carry him east in a hurry, and the only things he'd brought with him up to the rock were his rifle and ammunition.

He imagined himself shooting Slocum—that dastardly killer of his dreams!—and making a clean run to California free and clear. Actually, he'd be a free man once he crossed the county line—town sheriffs had a very limited range of authority, and he was aware of that. He thought of towns along the way that he'd heard of. One was Monkey Springs, which had undoubtedly been named by an idiot. But he believed that it must be the closest source for supplies.

Of course, murder was a capital crime, but he imagined that he could make himself over so that no one would recognize him. Grow a beard perhaps. Dye the gray out of his hair. Develop a limp.

He'd come up with something. He was a clever man.

He huddled down behind some brush growing from a crevice in the rocks, and waited.

Slocum excused himself, but he didn't go upstairs. Instead, he went to the kitchen. There, he found Sam and the others still at work, cleaning up the supper things.

He sat down, asking, "You ever send leftovers down to the hands?"

Sam looked up. She still had a glow in her cheeks from this afternoon, and Slocum felt himself flush. "Not normally, unless it's a holiday or somebody's birthday. But this evening I made extra for the boys, with Cookie's help." Smiling, she indicated a short, older man over by the sink.

"Cookie," Slocum said, nodding.

Cookie grunted back. Sam leaned close to Slocum, whispering, "That's about all he ever says to anybody. Consider yourself lucky."

A slow grin began to creep over Slocum's face. Hiram had himself quite an outfit, all right. He whispered back, "You about finished up down here?"

She replied, "Not for a while. Go on back and rest, if you like." Her eyes slid to meet his. "You'll need it."

He felt himself swallow hard. "If you don't cut that out," he said in a mock threat, "I'm gonna have to sit here until every last living soul leaves the kitchen."

"Really." She pursed her lips.

His pants got that much tighter. "Now cut that out!"

"Did you say something to me?" Thor looked up from the leftover roast he was carefully wrapping. Probably for their breakfast.

"No, Thor," Sam answered for Slocum. "We're just talking. When you put that roast away, bring me out a nice ham for tomorrow's breakfast, would you please?"

"Sure, sis," Thor replied, and got back to business.

He was tying up the bundle with string before Slocum said or did anything. Carefully, Slocum rose and stepped behind Sam's chair to hide himself. "I think I'll go try to catch a catnap," he said.

"Good night then, Slocum," she said without looking up. Her hands—and eyes—were busy with an enormous pile of snap beans.

"Night, Sam," he repeated. "Night, folks."

Several servants murmured, "Night, Mr. Slocum," and he managed to make it to the door without embarrassing himself. He leaned heavily against the wall outside in the servants' hall, and waited until he was comfortable enough to walk the few additional steps to Sam's room.

Hiram, drunk as a lord but trying his best not to show it, finally stopped talking long enough to realize something. "Goose!" he said, interrupting his own story. "Is that boy asleep?"

Goose lifted his own head. "Asleep? Who's asleep?"

Hiram set his snifter down precariously on the edge of his table. He leaned forward and pointed at Xander. "Him, that's who."

Goose, who was by that time roused enough to realize what was going on, said, "Yessir, I do believe he is there, Hiram." He reached across the space between their chairs and shook the boy's arm gently, taking care to remove the empty brandy snifter from his hand and set it aside more carefully than Hiram had his. "Xander? Xander, son, wake up and take yourself on upstairs."

Xander muttered something or other; then his eyes fluttered open. "Huh?" he said sleepily.

"I said, it's time you woke up enough to take yourself to bed. It's late."

"What time?" asked the boy, still blinking sleepily.

Goose looked around for a clock and couldn't find one, but Hiram looked past him and announced, "Nine thirty. You're right, Goose. It's getting to be about bedtime. Slocum left an hour ago!"

Hiram started another wide gesture with his hands, and Goose stopped him. "Watch your glass there, friend."

"Thank you, thank you," Hiram muttered. And then his face filled with emotion. "I don't know what I would'a done without you boys here to help me. I just don't know."

"That's all right, Hiram," Goose said. He had stood up and lifted Xander by one arm. With the other, he patted Hiram on the back. "I wouldn't'a wanted to miss meetin' up with you and your hospitality." Xander was gaining his own feet by then, which was a good thing because Goose was about to let him drop. A man—particularly a man who has imbibed almost half a bottle of Napoleon brandy—can't exactly keep up with more than one thing at a time.

"It's been a hoot and a boon to meet you, Goose," slurred Hiram. "Thank you so much. Thanks for gettin' here with Slocum."

"No trouble," Goose replied, suddenly standing erect as if he were on board a ship once again and before the captain. "No trouble at all, sir."

Xander fell against his side, and the two of them almost went down. But Goose kept them standing. "If you don't mind, believe we'll take our leave for the night, Hiram."

"Thank you," said Xander, although it was impossible to tell if he was speaking to Hiram or Goose.

But they both said, "You're welcome," in unison, then laughed about it.

"Who was he talkin' to?" Hiram slurred as Goose led Xander toward the door.

"Beats the hell outta me." With the arm not holding Xander up, Goose opened the door. If he'd had the strength, he would've rounded up Slocum and made him help get the kid upstairs. Xander was no toddler. "Night, Hiram," he said as he walked the boy out into the hallway.

"Night, everybody," said Hiram, and being in no mood to climb stairs, let alone remember names, he plopped down on the horsehair divan beneath the big front window. He made quite a racket doing it, but didn't notice.

He was asleep before he hit the couch.

Outside, Harvey Smollets had dozed off twice, and awakened himself both times. He kept his eyes on the upstairs windows, watching for any signs of life. Or to be more exact, any signs of Slocum.

He knew what to look for. Chip and Roy had filled him in there. He was looking for a big man—muscular, not fat—with dark brown hair. And "a way about him," whatever that meant. Chip had used the phrase twice, and Roy three times, while they were talking about the bastard. They said people wrote books about him.

"Literary taste has gone to the dogs since I was a lad," he muttered.

At long last, a light appeared at one of the downstairs windows. The landing for the stairs, he fervently hoped.

He was right. He watched that light fade as it grew in the third upstairs window, then made out the silhouettes of two large men, one helping the other, who seemed impaired. Smollets hoped so. He hoped whoever it was had taken a terribly bad fall from his horse, then been gored by one of the cattle that still had horns.

That would serve him right, wouldn't it?

The light disappeared from the window, then suddenly appeared in the next one. Someone must have opened the door. He watched as the first figure was unceremoniously dropped on the bed—at least, he hoped there was a bed there. His vision was limited because of the position of the lantern, and the figures appeared to him in silhouette.

He didn't feel that Slocum was the one being deposited on the bed. He was big enough, all right, but Slocum didn't seem like a fellow foolish enough to fall off his horse and hurt himself.

Through the sights on the rifle, Smollets took careful aim at the other figure, a big, wide-shouldered man walking away from the window and toward the door.

Smollets took a deep breath and held it in, steadying himself.

He fired.

The explosion of bullet shattering glass, followed by the loud clump and thud of Goose falling to the floor, failed to wake Hiram, but it got Slocum's attention. Whispering, "Sorry, baby," to Sam, he left her on the bed, climbed into his britches, and headed toward the sound.

He raced through the dining room, then the parlor and the front hall and the billiards room, before he got to the base of the stairs and started up. Someone was lying on the floor outside Xander's room, someone big, but Slocum wasn't sure who it was until he had climbed halfway up the stairs and Xander appeared groggily in the doorway.

"Goose?" asked Slocum.

Xander, who seemed to have just come to the realization

that someone had been shot, suddenly yelped, "My pa!" and dropped to his knees beside the body. Slocum arrived around the same time he hit the floor.

"Is he dead?" Xander squeaked, a little drunkenly. And then he shouted at the body, "You can't be dead, you son-ofabitch! I just found you!" He began to weep openly.

Slocum pushed him roughly aside and put an ear to Goose's chest, then fingers to his neck. "He's alive," he said, and not without a good deal of gratitude. He had really gotten to like old Goose during their short acquaintance.

Slocum said, "Get his feet," to the boy, then lifted Goose's shoulders up off the floor. Together, they carried him to his bed. Slocum began to tear at his shirt, ripping it away to expose a gaping bullet wound in his chest.

"Jesus," he muttered. "What'd they use? A buffalo gun?"

While he was complaining and washing the wound, the servants began to arrive and Zelda, the first one there, saw what had happened and raced for their medical kit.

When she returned, Slocum had the room cleared except for Thor—who was then given orders to ride to town for the doctor—and began to probe for the slug. It had buried itself in Goose's shoulder, not his lung or his heart—as Slocum had first feared—but it would be a bitch to get out of there. Fortunately, Goose had passed out long before Slocum pulled the bullet clear and deposited it in Xander's palm.

Xander stared at the bloody, misshapen slug. "What am I supposed to do with it?"

"Clean it up. He might wanna keep it to remember how close he came to meetin' the Grim Reaper."

Xander nodded. "Oh. Okay."

"Bring me some more rags, kid. I can't get this bleeding stopped."

Indeed, more blood than ever was now freely flowing from the wound, and Slocum had decided that enough rags and pressure would hold it down until the doc got there to stitch Goose up.

Xander shot from the room to find more rags, and Hiram, apparently awakened by the servants, stumbled in the door. "Whass goin' on?" he asked imperiously, and promptly fell sideways into the seat of a chair. "Somebody get hurt or somethin'? How dare they, in my house!"

"Goose has been shot," Slocum said, ignoring his employer's drunken state. He was trying to stave off the bleeding with already soaked rags, and having little luck. He wished he'd sent somebody for Apollo, too. Somebody had to ride for the sheriff over at the Smollets place.

But Apollo seemed to have read his mind, because just then, Slocum heard boots coming up the stairs and thumping quickly down the hall. Apollo stuck his head into the room. "Somebody shoot Goose?"

Slocum nodded. "Came from out there." He pointed across the hall. "Took out Xander's window, too."

"My window," muttered Hiram drunkenly.

Sam appeared, pushing Apollo aside so that she could carry in some fresh rags. She handed half to Slocum, then sat on the other side of the bed, folding the rest into bandages.

To Apollo, Slocum said, "Can you roust somebody out and get hold of the sheriff or chase this guy down or somethin'? He can't have got very far yet."

Apollo nodded curtly, then disappeared into the hall. Slocum heard his boots clattering down the stairway.

The fresh rags were helping, and Sam moved Slocum's away to apply hers, which were quite a bit more effective. "You gotta apply pressure. Even, constant pressure," he explained. He knew about wounds, having received more than his fair share, and having been awake for the doctoring of most of them.

She nodded. "Like this?"

"Perfect," he replied, then grinned. "'Fraid you're gonna live to see that long trek back, Goose. Yessir, I believe you are."

When he looked up, Samantha was smiling down at Goose, too. And Hiram, flopped over the chair across the room, began to snore. Xander, leaned up against the doorway, slowly slid to the ground and snored as well.

20

Slocum shook his head. "We can't have that. The kid's got to be put to bed." Then, realizing that there was no one else there capable, he said, "Sam, keep up holding the pressure. I'm gonna put the kid in bed."

She nodded. "Check the bed for glass first."

"Yup."

Slocum hooked Xander beneath his armpits, then dragged him across the hall. The shooter had surely done a job on his window. The lower pane was shattered completely. But it hadn't helped Goose escape.

Through it, he saw lights flickering over by the rocks, and slung the boy into a chair by the door to investigate. The lights, he saw once he went to the window, were torches in the hands of Hiram's men, searching the rocks—and around them—for evidence of their shooter.

Then somebody shouted, "Here!" and the torches converged back behind the outcrop, so that all Slocum could see was a glow.

Then he heard the muddle of several men speaking at once, and then they mounted up, torches held high, and galloped off in a straggly line toward the west. They'd found a trail then. Slocum smirked, then went back to Xander's chair. Which the boy had managed to slide out of.

"Aw, hell," Slocum grumbled, then went back to the bed and pulled off the bedspread. Seemed the kid hadn't had the strength—or the presence of mind—to get into the bed, only on it. So, stripping off the spread would take care of any glass that had landed on it. And quite a bit had, he judged by the tinkle and pop when he threw the spread to the floor.

Then he finally went back, dragged the kid to the bed, and rolled him into it. More like onto it. He snugged a pillow under Xander's neck, whispered, "Night, kid," then returned to Goose's room.

Sam greeted him with, "No change."

"Good. At least he's not gettin' any worse." Slocum sat down in the straight-back chair he'd occupied before, and put his head in his hands. He rubbed at his forehead.

"You're gonna need another shower bath when this is over."

Slocum looked up. "Huh?"

"You're a mess, my dear," she said with a smile.

He looked down at his hands, with which he'd just rubbed his forehead. They were red with Goose's blood. He'd gotten a good bit on his shirtfront, too. She was right.

He said, "Yes'm."

Sam smiled, and he returned it. He asked her, "How long you figure before the doc gets here?"

"Depends," she said. "On whether he's out on a case somewhere, and on whether he's drunk. If he's sober and in town—two very large ifs—then it shouldn't be much longer. Maybe another half hour, depending on who Apollo sent to town." She checked Goose's wound again. When she peeked under the bandage, the blood began flowing at its old rate again. "Damn," she breathed as she pressed the rags down again. "If he sent Bodie, it might be sooner."

When Slocum arched a brow, she added, "He works for Hiram, and he's got the territorial champion quarter-mile horse."

All this time, Slocum had been in the presence of greatness and hadn't known it! He said, "When we get time, and when it's not the middle of the freakin' night, I wanna meet this Bodie. And his horse."

Sam smiled. "You will. I'm sure he'll be up to the house for the wedding."

"And when's that?"

"Tomorrow afternoon, if the circuit rider gets here as expected."

"Does he usually?" Slocum asked. "Get here when he's expected, I mean."

Sam nodded, and Slocum felt a little better. If the doc was absent or drunk, at least they'd have somebody official handy to pray for Goose.

Bodie Crane rousted out the doctor, waking him up enough to understand what had happened out at the Walker spread, then rushed him outside to get his rig ready. However, after looking at the doc's old buggy horse, he said, "Here, take mine instead. Move it! A man's bleedin' to death!" And he handed over his horse's reins.

Handing his Sprint over to a stranger wasn't something that Bodie was accustomed to doing, so once he got the doc's old pony harnessed to the buggy, he laid into him, jangling the lanterns suspended from the rig, trying to make it back to the ranch as soon as possible.

Doc wasn't a bad rider, but he wasn't a good one either. He made it to the Walking W about ten minutes before Bodie pulled in—but in that ten minutes, the doctor managed to clamp off the bleeder and save Goose's life.

As he continued to work on Goose, Slocum had gone on downstairs, arriving in time to take a look at Bodie's horse, which Doc had tied to the porch. He was nice-looking, Slocum thought. He had a big, round butt—no fat, all muscle—sturdy feet and legs, and a mighty shoulder. His neck came up smooth from his withers, and ended in a Roman-nosed head. Slocum would have liked to take him for a spin, but not without the owner's permission.

Just then, a growing rattle and thumping sound grew closer, and Slocum knew that Bodie was at hand. The doc's buggy pulled up in front of the house, and the yellow-haired kid Slocum had seen around the place jumped out, carrying a tie-weight to the horse's head.

"Bodie?" he asked.

The kid looked up. "You're Slocum, right?"

"Yup. This is a mighty fine horse you've got here. I don't usually favor roans, but like my daddy used to say, ain't no such thing as a bad color on a good horse."

Bodie smiled. "My daddy used to say the same thing. How's the patient? How long ago did Doc get here anyhow?"

Slocum grinned. "Patient's gonna make it. Doc got the bleeding stopped fine, and he's stitchin' him up now. And about ten minutes ago."

Bodie took off his hat and slapped it against his leg as hard as he could, or so it appeared to Slocum. "Goddammit! Don't anybody know how to ride anymore?" he ranted. "He should'a beat me by a good twenty minutes, and I was pushin' his old oater."

"Calm down, son," Slocum soothed. "He got the job done, and that's what counts. And your horse here—"

"Sprint."

"And Sprint here didn't dump him. I'd say that was pretty good for an emergency."

Bodie bent to check his horse's legs and feet. "You're ridin' that big Appy, ain't you?"

"Yeah. The liver chestnut."

"Nice horse."

"Thanks. Where'd you get Sprint?"

At last, Bodie finished checking the horse over, and he stood up. "Down to Bisbee. Bought him off a trader when he wasn't even a yearling." He smiled. "Traded an old army bugle, my Great Aunt Zoe's old wedding ring—made outta Nevada silver—and a Navaho rug for him. Think I got the best of the deal."

Slocum nodded. "I believe you did, son. I believe you did."

After the doc was finished and had taken his leave, and everybody left on the ranch had finally gotten to bed, Sam and Slocum took a shower, but didn't get much farther than that. They both fell into her bed and went promptly to sleep. They didn't rise until early the next morning, when Apollo came riding in with the rest of the hands. He was leading a bound and gagged Harvey Smollets.

Slocum met him on the porch. "This here's our shooter?" he asked.

Apollo nodded, frowning. "Harvey Smollets, meet Slocum." Smollets growled, and Slocum sent him a dirty look. "Picked up his tracks over on the other side of the road, then followed him on down to Monkey Springs. Or a little outside of it. He was burnin' leather, but we were a mite more pissed than he was."

Slocum smiled a little. "Good for you, Apollo. Couldn't have done it better myself." And then he realized how that sounded, and added, "Well, you know what I mean."

Apollo laughed, and Smollets, who was still gagged, snarled at him. A snarl that Slocum was pretty sure included *him*.

Apollo said, "Gonna take him to his ranch if the sheriff's still there."

Slocum nodded. "Imagine he is. He's gotta wait on a whole mess of ranchers to come pick up their thieved cattle. You look wore out, Apollo. Why don't you tie him up in a stall or the tack room or someplace and come have some breakfast? Let your horse have a little breather, too."

Apollo agreed, and fifteen minutes later was sitting in the kitchen with Slocum and Sam. Apollo appeared tired enough to doze off right there in his chair, but the smell of Sam's scrambled eggs and bacon kept his eyes open and his mouth watering. Once she served him those, she cut off a slice of ham and set it to frying while she made him some toast in the oven.

"By God, you folks sure eat good up here at the big house," he said around a mouthful of bacon and eggs. Sam slid a plate of butter and a pot of cactus jelly on the table.

"And all the time," Slocum replied, with not a little wonder in his voice. "Between you and me, I think Hiram must secretly be the king of somewhere or other."

"No," Sam offered as she refilled Apollo's coffee. "But his wife is."

Slocum grinned. "King?"

She smiled back. "No, queen. Her family practically owns Wall Street."

Apollo screwed up his face. "Wall Street?"

She said simply, "They have a lot of money."

Slocum shook his head as he waited for Apollo to start eating. He had been taught to wait for everyone else before he dug into vittles. "They surely must have," was all he said.

21

Apollo had been gone from the kitchen for ten minutes when Slocum heard him outside, shouting, "He's gone! Everybody start lookin'!"

Slocum broke off the kiss he was planting on Samantha's elbow and was out the kitchen door like a shot. He raced through the house to the front door, and when he arrived, there were men scurrying everywhere. And Apollo was coming out of the toolshed, half carrying Smollets before him.

"Don't none'a you idiots know how to tie a goddamn knot?" he shouted. He shoved Smollets forward again. After each step, Smollets put on the brakes, making their progress across the yard difficult. It also made Apollo that much madder.

Slocum stepped down off the porch and went to help. He figured if they each took an arm, they could haul Smollets up off his feet and take him to Des Moines, Iowa, if they wanted to.

But Smollets had other ideas.

When Slocum got close enough to grab Smollets's left arm, the little weasel moved almost impossibly fast and lifted Apollo's gun.

Apollo jumped and slapped at his holster, shouting, "You turd!"

And before he could reach around to pull the smaller pistol he carried in the back of his belt, Smollets had already drawn a bead on Slocum. He snarled, "Move any further and I'll kill him, you half-breed lout!"

Apollo froze.

Slocum was already still, his hands just inches away from his cross-draw rig—he'd put it on first thing this morning, for which he promised to thank the Lord, once he had the time.

If he had the time. And the breath.

To Apollo, he said, "That a Smith & Wesson?"

Apollo furrowed his brow. "Yeah, why?" Quickly, he glanced over at Smollets, then back to Slocum.

"Old one?"

"Shut up, you heathen!" hollered Smollets.

And then, understanding spread over Apollo's dark-complected face. He said, "Real old. Daddy had it before the Civil War."

"Thanks," Slocum said, and quickly drew his gun, shooting Smollets in the shoulder. He dropped the pistol when he fell, and Slocum kicked it over toward Apollo. Applause and whistles broke out from the hands who had ducked behind the water troughs and hidden behind barn and outbuilding doors.

Slocum continued. "You see, Mr. Smollets—or can I call you Harvey?—those old Smith & Wessons gotta be cocked afore you can fire 'em. This," he added, pointing to his own gun, "is a Colt pistol, not more'n a year old. It's a single-action." He holstered the gun and stood back while a mob of Apollo's crew swarmed in to bind the wounded Smollets.

Smollets cried out at the rough handling, but Slocum said to the men, "You don't have to mind that shoulder too much. I only hit him in the meat."

"Get that bastard up on a horse," Apollo demanded. "Now, before I stick a gun up his ass and shoot him into the saddle."

It crossed Slocum's mind that he wouldn't like to have Apollo mad at him.

"Lucky thing I had that Smith & Wesson for him to grab," Apollo said, holstering it.

"You're not just whistlin' Dixie," Slocum replied. He glanced back at the house, and saw Sam and Thor and Nils, along with Xander and Hiram, lining the porch. "At least we provided folks with some entertainment."

"Entertainment!" Smollets shouted just before Bodie slipped on a gag.

"Jess, bring my horse out," Apollo shouted. "Bodie, you're gonna make the trip to town with me, seeing as you're the one who's had the most sleep. Is Smollets's nag still saddled?"

As Apollo went on ordering men about, Slocum walked on back to the house and climbed up on the porch.

"Holy whiskers!" was the first thing out of Xander's mouth, and Sam ran to Slocum, hugging him tight.

She said, "How? He had the drop on you!"

"I'll explain it later," he said, "I promise. Now go fix me some breakfast, woman." He swatted her behind, and she laughed.

"Will someone tell me what's going on?" Hiram demanded groggily. Apparently, he'd been the last one outside.

"In time, in time," said Slocum, and walked past everybody into the house.

A little later, over breakfast, Slocum explained the morning's goings-on to Hiram, and at last he was satisfied. Goose, being bedridden for the time being, had his breakfast served in bed. It was obviously something he wasn't used to, because he accused Mary, who brought up his tray, of trying to be nice to him because she didn't think he'd last the day.

Even in his weakened condition, it took both her and Nils to sit on him for a good hour before he finally gave in and ate. Mary said that when they'd left him, he'd emptied the tray and was sound asleep.

"He's one tough old bird," Slocum said with a smile.

Xander grinned. "Thanks, Slocum!"

"Yeah, you be sure to tell him," Slocum replied with a smirk.

But Xander took him seriously. "Oh, I will!"

It was after breakfast, and they had joined Hiram in his study for his mid-morning brandy, which turned out to be sherry instead. Xander didn't have much of a taste for it, but Slocum drank the boy's glass, too.

Hiram was just pouring out a third glass—for himself— when someone knocked at the door. A few moments later, Nils showed the circuit rider, Reverend Julian Connor, into the room. Introductions were made all around, and Slocum had a good chance to look him over and study the cut of his jib, so to speak.

He was a tall, spare man, as lean as Hiram was portly,

and clean-shaven, with long, curly, graying hair that hung down his back. His accent wasn't local, but Irish, as if he'd just come over from the old country.

"'Scuse me, Reverend Connor, but why ain't you Catholic?" Slocum asked once they'd all had a chance to sit down and relax.

The reverend laughed. "By heaven, that's the first time anyone's had the stones to ask me that very question! I'm Protestant, Mr. Slocum, because my whole family is Protestant, and because we come from the north of the country. You'll find it differs elsewhere."

Grinning, Slocum said, "So my pappy told me. I guess they got quite some argument goin' on over there."

"Indeed, indeed," said Reverend Connor. "Me own brother was killed in a street brawl between Protestant and Catholic gangs." He frowned and shook his head. "'Tis a terrible thing, the taking of lives, when it's the same God we all worship and his same Son that we all revere."

Slocum nodded solemnly. When he was a child, he remembered his father talking about the "troubles" in the old country. He was saddened to hear that they were still going on.

"Now," said Hiram, who apparently didn't care much for the troubles of Ireland, "what about this wedding?"

Reverend Connor tipped his head. "What wedding?"

Slocum said, "Sorry, Julian. Guess it got forgot in all this talk about the old sod. Hiram here has a couple of servants who're countin' on you hitchin' 'em today."

"Thor's father's coming," Xander volunteered. "But not Zelda's family. They're too far away."

"Thanks, Xander," Slocum said. "When's Thor's daddy supposed to get here?"

Xander barely managed to get his mouth open when he was interrupted by another knock on the door. "Now, I guess," he said, smiling smugly.

A few moments later, a grinning Nils showed his father into the study. Sven favored both his sons greatly, and Slocum could see a bit of Samantha in there, too. He, like the reverend, favored a gray beard, but his was not as well groomed as the reverend's. He was dressed as if he were going to Sunday meeting. Even his boots were spit-shined.

"Vell, hello, hello dere!" he boomed once Nils had introduced him to everyone. And then he shook hands with the reverend once again, and asked, "Vat denomination are you? You're not Cat'lic, are you?"

"No, afraid there's not a touch of purple on me. I'm a plain, simple boyo. Church of England."

Sven nodded his head and stroked his beard. "Dat's fine wit me, I'm guessin'." He looked at Hiram. "Vere you keepin' my boy and his little flicka?"

Hiram gestured at Nils, who had remained inside the room, standing by the door. "Nils can show you," he said.

"Vell, den," said Sven, rising, "I tink I go see dem."

And without further ado, he left everyone else behind, tagging on Nils's heels. Slocum heard his booming voice all the way back to the kitchen, although he couldn't make out any words through the man's thick accent. Well, of course, he was talking to Nils. Maybe they were conversing in Swedish or Norwegian or something.

It seemed like a good time for Slocum to take his leave, so he said, "Hiram, you mind if I take a glass of sherry up to Goose?"

Hiram suddenly seemed appalled at his own bad manners. "Certainly not, certainly not! I should have thought of it myself!" He rose and poured a double sherry, then handed the glass to Slocum, who was on his feet, too. Xander was taking advantage of the situation, and was already standing beside the open door, waiting for Slocum.

"I thank you, and Goose thanks you, Hiram," Slocum said as he crossed the room. "Been an honor, Reverend. We'll see you at the service."

"Most welcome!" said Hiram as the Reverend Connor nodded. "But the wedding's not until after lunch!"

"Then we'll see you over another of Hiram's good spreads. They're the finest kind!"

Slocum and Xander left the room.

Apollo, despite his exhaustion, rode into the farmyard at a canter, leapt off his horse, and threw his reins around the hitching rail. He practically vaulted up on the porch and started knocking on the door. Hiram answered it himself, and when Apollo told him the news, he nearly fainted.

Leaving Hiram hanging onto the door and muttering, "Good God!" over and over, he bolted up the stairs and found Goose's room, where Slocum was slouched in a hard-backed chair, and Xander sat on the end of the bed.

He burst inside so quickly that Slocum, saying, "What is it?" climbed halfway to his feet before Apollo motioned him back down.

"It's Smollets," he said, panting. He leaned against the door's frame.

"Did he escape again?" asked Xander, moving toward the edge of the bed.

Apollo shook his head and waved his hand. Xander stopped moving.

"Then what?" asked Goose, who had just been filled in on the morning's goings-on. Despite the amount of pain he must be in, he sat forward. Concern was written on his face.

"He was wanted for more than cattle rustlin'," Apollo said. "Slocum, he killed Mrs. Richards last night at the jail, and he set all his buddies free."

"Killed?" Slocum asked, his brows shooting up. "Who's Mrs. Richards?"

"The old lady that cooks for the jail. And I only know that because one'a Smollets's men came back. Last night, I mean."

"To do what?"

"To lock himself back up," Apollo answered with a shrug. "It was that blond kid. Milo somethin'-or-other. I had to lock Smollets in the cell farthest away from him. I thought he was gonna kill him when the kid told me what happened."

Slocum shook his head. "You stop and tell the sheriff on the way back?"

Apollo nodded. "He left a few men to watch over what cattle are still waitin' to be picked up and went hightailin' it back to town." He dropped his head for a moment, then looked up again. "Slocum, he could'a killed you this mornin'."

Slocum grunted. "Could'a killed quite a few of us, sounds like. It sure would'a cut down the guest list for the weddin' this afternoon."

Goose laughed, then clutched his shoulder in pain, and Xander moved to his side.

"Yeah," Apollo said, smiling a little for the first time. "It sure would'a."

22

Lunch came and went, and an hour later, the wedding was set up in the parlor. It was a grand room indeed. Hiram confided that his wife only used it on rare occasions. Before, Slocum and Xander had gone upstairs to help Goose downstairs, so that he could be a part of the festivities, and they had seated him in a comfortable chair at the back of the room.

Samantha played the piano, which Hiram said had been constructed in Germany, shipped all the way to Corpus Christi, Texas, then carted out to him by wagon train. She played beautifully, and Sven nodded in time to the "Wedding March."

The groom appeared, looking dapper, if slightly uncomfortable, in one of Hiram's good suits from the old days, when he was considerably slimmer, and the bride was attired in a new beige dress, with a crown of flowers on her head—flowers that Slocum had glimpsed Sam cutting in the garden earlier.

Reverend Connor spoke his bit with clear warmth and sincerity, and the happy couple was married. Slocum noticed that when it was time for Zelda to toss the bouquet, Sam made a point of not grabbing for it. The flowers were caught by Mary, who then made eyes at a blushing Nils.

Xander saw that look, too, and stared down at his boots in disappointment.

Slocum and all the men convened on the back porch for lemonade and cake—chocolate, iced with peppermint, at Zelda and Thor's request—and eventually, Samantha and Mary, plus a couple of housemaids, joined them on the porch. Likely out of desperation. There were no other women there.

But soon enough, the lemonade was laced with whiskey, then the whiskey was laced with lemonade, and then the lemonade disappeared, as did the women. When it came time for the evening meal, the bride and groom had already departed for a Tucson honeymoon, the hands had gone down to the bunkhouse, Goose was carried back upstairs, and the Reverend Connor and Sven joined Hiram, Slocum, and Xander at the table. The five of them were drunk as lords—Slocum and the reverend the least, and Hiram the most—and the first half hour was taken up with toasting. Mostly by Hiram.

Samantha had prepared a standing rib roast with browned potatoes and carrots and onions surrounding it like a moat, plus a surfeit of side dishes. But as good as the meal was—and it was outstanding—all Slocum wanted to do was lie down. Xander beat him to it and fell asleep at the table, his face in his plate.

Afterward, Slocum excused himself and Xander, not wishing to spend another brandy-soaked evening with Hiram. He wanted to keep at least part of his wits about him, for he knew Sam was waiting for him. Reverend Connor went upstairs, too, after blessing them all, and retired to his guest room. But Sven, who seemed to have a hollow leg when it came to spirits, went with Hiram to the study. And the bar.

After seeing that Xander got to bed and checking on Goose, who was just being relieved of his dinner tray by Nils, Slocum went down the back stairs to the kitchen. There, he found his Sam, helping Mary with the dishes.

"Quite the festivities," he remarked as he slid into a chair at the table.

"They certainly were," Sam replied, grinning. She had to talk over her shoulder or she'd drop a plate. "You gents certainly seemed to have a fine time. I swan, I don't know where Hiram keeps the liquor locked up, but he's got an endless supply of it."

Just then, Nils came in the back hall door, carrying Goose's pillaged dinner tray. "He says to tell you it was a 'right good spread,' Samantha," Nils said as he set the tray at Mary's elbow. "Hello again, Mr. Slocum."

"Nils." Slocum nodded. "That daddy of your's is a bottomless pit!"

Nils grinned. "Think he misses Sam's cookin'."

Slocum had meant the booze, but he just nodded and said, "He sure liked that weddin' cake, didn't he? Four pieces that I counted. 'Course, as the father of the groom, he's allowed whatever he wants. But four pieces?"

Nils broke out into a smile. "Six. I counted. At home, Sam'd always bake us two cakes at a time. One for Pa and one for the rest of us."

"And that's the truth," Sam said from across the room, and Slocum laughed.

*   *   *

By ten o'clock, everybody was settled in for the night, if not fast asleep, but Slocum and Sam were just getting down to business.

He ran his hand through her long hair, brushing it away from her face, then tilted her face toward him. She was so beautiful! He kissed her gently, then deeply, and she returned the kiss urgently, needily. Before either of them knew it, they were naked and together on Samantha's bed, and she was running those long, delicate fingers up Slocum's legs, tracing the scars from Apache spears and Yuma knives, the scars from guns and rifles and whips and spurs, all the while moving upward toward his crotch.

He didn't need to tell her what to do next. Her mouth lowered to his manhood and she took him, fully erect, into her mouth. Slocum gasped and reached down to take her hand. "Yes," he breathed.

She squeezed his hand, then broke the contact to grip the base of his shaft, an effort that took both her hands. She began to lick and nibble and suck at him, alternately taking him deep into her wet, warm mouth, then sliding him nearly out, her tongue tickling, then laving at the head, and then back in, repeating it until he was almost crazed with fever for her.

He reached for her, amazed at the effort it took him to move. "Sam," he tried to say. "Sam, stop before—"

And then it was too late. His loins suddenly exploded, and he felt his hips move up into the air like a bucking bronc—with her still attached, finishing him off masterfully.

When she slipped off him and slowly made her way up his chest, kissing every scar, sucking at his nipples, licking at the wide cords of his neck, and splaying her fingers across his broad chest, he was still without words. He only knew he was hard again, and this time he was going to take her.

Suddenly, he grabbed her by the shoulders and twisted them both over, so that now he was in control. "It's my turn, Sammy," he whispered. She smiled, then kissed him—kissed him so thoroughly and so passionately that, for a moment, his lips and tongue became the center of his universe.

He let her do it. He loved this kind of bed-play, but he knew she must be aching for a release even more than he was. And he intended to give it to her.

While they were still engaged in kissing, he stealthily slipped both of his knees between hers, then moved her legs apart. Her kisses became more fevered. She knew what was coming.

Or thought she did.

He pushed himself forward until he was just outside the opening of her core, and then he pulled away, breaking off the kiss, ignoring her pleas of "No, Slocum!" He sat back on his heels and pulled her legs up, sliding her pretty backside along his thighs until he was deeply imbedded in her, and she gasped in surprise and pleasure. Then he pulled her knees up until they were bent over his shoulders, with her feet dangling down his back.

He began to move. Not slowly. Not this time. With her lower body on his thighs, he began to thrust into her for all he was worth, hammering himself home with every push. Her hands tore at the bed linens; her head moved from side to side. She kept mouthing something, something frantic and animal, but he couldn't understand. He was caught up in the moment, too.

And then he felt himself begin to rise, felt his juices bubbling and steaming, and came in a huge jolting thrust.

Two more thrusts and he was done. And so was she. Wide-eyed, she stared up at him, panting wildly, her inner contractions tugging at him. "I never . . ." she said, "I never . . ."

He pulled out of her and slumped to the expanse of bed beside her. "Now you have," he said, brushing her open mouth with a kiss.

They slept soundly through the night, exhausted.

Come about ten the next morning, Sheriff Black rode in, looking grim. Slocum was down at the horse barn, seeing to Speck's hooves, and came out to meet him.

He put up his hand. "Mornin'! What brings you out here?"

The sheriff dismounted. "Bad news, I'm afraid." Without further prompting from Slocum, the sheriff went on simply. "Harvey Smollets is out again."

Slocum's brow creased. "What?"

"He's out. Banged the deputy bringin' him breakfast over the head this morning and run off. Got deputies scourin' half the territory for him right now, but he holds that rustlin' charge against you, Slocum. He's tried for you once. He'd have to be pretty stupid to do it, but you ought'a know he's out and might try again."

"Obliged you told me," Slocum allowed with a nod.

The sheriff nodded back. "No problem. Believe I'll go on down to the bunkhouse, tell the boys to keep their eyes open. Apollo down there?"

"Think so," Slocum replied. And as an afterthought, he shouted, "You're stayin' for lunch, ain't you?" at Sheriff Black's retreating back.

The sheriff turned around and shouted, "Are you kiddin'? 'Course I'm stayin'!"

Still smiling, Slocum returned to the barn and picked up Speck's off hind hoof. He began to pick it, thinking how funny it was that when folks stopped at Hiram's, they usually did it at meal time. He shook his head. Sam must be famous or something.

Her father, Sven, was leaving after lunch, too. So far this morning, he'd split his time between the kitchen and Hiram's study. Drinking and eating seemed to be the way he celebrated, and he was surely celebrating up a storm! Reverend Connor was staying over a couple of days to tend to the folks in the countryside around Hiram's ranch. Hiram's table fare seemed to attract the Lord's work as well.

Additionally, one of the neighbors had ridden in at about nine—one apparently not interested in a meal—had a few words with Hiram, then handed Slocum an envelope. "I wanna say thanks, Slocum," he said simply. "God bless you. We got back over three hundred head."

Slocum took the envelope from him and nodded his thanks, but didn't think to open it until the fellow had ridden out. Inside, he found four hundred dollars, and had to sit down before he fell down.

"What the hell?" he asked Hiram.

"I told you to wait. I'm sure there'll be more."

"But I already been paid!"

"Not so far as these ranchers are concerned," said Hiram. "Some of those cows got stolen three or four years ago. And they've been calvin' every year since. Fellas figure they owe you for the offspring plus the feed. 'Course," he added, with a signature "Hiram" grin, "they ain't gonna pay you market price."

"But I—"

"You just wait and see, Slocum."

23

The lunch table was filled nearly to capacity. At least, without the extra table leaves inserted.

Goose had healed enough to get himself downstairs, although at about a fourth of his former rate. Slocum and Xander and Hiram were there, of course, plus Reverend Connor. Also, Sheriff Black was present, plus one of the neighbors, Vernon something-or-other. Vernon had handed Slocum an envelope containing money: two hundred dollars. It seemed he figured his cows weren't worth as much as the first man's, but Slocum was grateful anyway. A buck was a buck, and an extra buck was a boon.

He figured to wait till they left Hiram's, then split the money between himself, Goose, and Xander. In the meantime, he was salting his money away at the back of his bureau drawer, under a mousetrap.

He would've put it down his boot, but he figured that even Goose might be offended by that.

After lunch, the reverend ministered to Vernon's needs

and the sheriff rode back to town. Going upstairs proved to be beyond Goose's ability in his weakened state, so Slocum and Xander were called upon to help him on his way—with a little side trip to the study, of course.

Slocum could only shake his head at Hiram. What he drank each day likely would've killed any other man had he drunk it in a week!

Although asked to stay, Xander and Slocum declined, and went out to the porch instead. They pulled up a couple of rockers and sat down.

"Nice day," Slocum remarked.

"Hot," Xander replied.

Slocum raised a brow and snorted out a laugh. "What'd you expect?"

Xander smiled and shrugged his shoulders. "Hot, I guess." And then, after a moment, he said, "Maybe I shouldn't be pesterin' you about it, but . . . Do you miss havin' me for your son?"

Slocum had been half expecting it, but he was still taken aback by the question. He said, "I reckon I do sometimes. Goose is a lucky man, havin' a boy like you."

"Thanks," said Xander. "I mean, thanks for him. 'Cause he ain't here to say it, I mean. Aw, hell."

Slocum said, "Stop rockin' for a minute."

When he did, Slocum leaned over and gave him a quick hug. "You don't never need to get tongue-tied around me, boy. I was your pa once," he said with a smile. "Remember that."

Xander grinned and hugged Slocum back so hard, he thought his ribs were about to crack. "Easy, Xander! Don't crush the life outta your former pa!"

Xander let go immediately. "Sorry!" he said, looking embarrassed. "Guess I don't know my own strength!"

"That's puttin' it mildly," said Slocum, feigning a coughing fit for the boy's sake. It worked.

"Let's go back inside," Xander said, looking concerned. "You can sit in one of those soft chairs in the parlor."

Xander had risen, but chuckling, Slocum waved him back down. "I'm a little tender, but I ain't dead yet."

"Sorry."

"No need to be sorry, boy." He pointed out toward the far horizon where a small cloud of dust was rising. "Thought Hiram said he had the hands take his cows up the other way. Out toward the west."

Xander's brow furrowed. "He did."

"Must be riders then," said Slocum, hoping it was another happy—and grateful—rancher.

By the next afternoon, there'd been no sign of Smollets, but four more ranchers had turned up, bringing Slocum amounts from fifty dollars to five hundred. The man who gave him fifty dollars was scruffy with torn clothes, and had only picked up twenty-two head. Slocum tried to make him take his fifty bucks back, but the man insisted, and Slocum finally gave up.

Cord Whipple had been by, too, leaving a thick wad of bills in a manila envelope.

Slocum figured that counting Hiram's money, he'd have over $3200 to split up with Xander and Goose, plus the four hundred he intended to leave as a tip for the servants. Well, two hundred for Sam, and the others could split up the rest. A damn good two or three days' work, if you asked him. Plus, Goose and Xander'd have a split of the reward money.

If the authorities ever got Smollets back in jail, that is. This was looking more unlikely with every passing hour.

All in all, Slocum hated to think of leaving Hiram behind. Well, not Hiram exactly, but Sam—her body and her cooking and just her sweet little self—but he knew that as soon as Goose could travel, they'd have to hit the trail. The killer or killers of Goose's brother and nephew were still on the loose, and that needed to be remedied.

And just how soon would that be?

He decided to take a hike upstairs and check with Goose.

Slocum pulled out a chair and sat by Goose's bed. "You're lookin' chipper," he said with a grin.

Goose was. He said, "And the top'a the mornin' to you, Slocum! Or is it the top of the afternoon yet?"

"Reverend Connor been spendin' a lot of time in here?" Slocum asked,

"How could you tell?"

Slocum laughed. "I've got my ways. I come to ask when you might feel up to travelin'."

Goose studied on that for a moment. "Maybe the day after tomorrow," he said finally, "if the road ain't too rugged."

Slocum nodded. "That can be arranged, buddy."

Goose said, "Fine. The sooner Bill and Badger's killer gets stopped, the better."

"Agreed," said Slocum, and rose out of his chair. "You rest up and I'll see you later."

"Wait a minute."

Slocum turned back toward him. "What?"

"Been meanin' to ask you. How's your neck?"

Slocum laughed. "You mean, where you shot me?"

Goose nodded.

Slocum felt the back of his neck. "Most'a the scab's gone. Gonna have another nice scar."

"Sorry," Goose muttered.

"You ought'a be," Slocum teased. "Another fraction of an inch, and I'd be pushin' up sagebrush."

Goose grinned a little. "Sorry I was such a good shot. I s'pose if it'd been a fraction the other way, it would'a missed you entire."

"That's what they tell me."

"Lucky my aim was off."

The day after tomorrow arrived sooner than anyone expected, and Slocum, Goose, and Xander made ready to leave. First, they'd ride back up to Lonesome, and then they'd start asking questions. A lot of very uncomfortable questions.

Sam had been cooking and cooking, presenting them with enough parcels to weigh their horses down. Slocum was concerned about carrying water, too, but Hiram presented him with a pack mule. While Xander busied himself moving the food from the horses to the mule, Hiram put off Slocum's protestations.

"Don't be an idiot," Hiram said. "Consider it a tip. One well-deserved tip!"

Xander and Goose filled the water bags, slung them on their horses and the mule, and then they were all set for desert traveling. Xander and Goose made quite a pair. Slocum had gotten over his doubts about giving up the boy. He was with his real father now, and that was what mattered.

But Sam mattered, too. He slipped inside the house for a second, found her in the kitchen, and took her in his arms. "Good-bye, baby," he said just before he kissed her.

She surprised him, after he broke off the kiss, by turning in his arms so that her back was to him. "Just go, Slocum," she said.

"Sam?" He walked around to face her. "What's'a matter, honey? You knew I was goin'. I told you—"

She put a hand in the middle of his chest. "I know, I know. It's just that sometimes the reality is harder than the *idea* of the reality. You know?"

Although she'd halfway lost him, Slocum nodded and said, "Yeah."

She sniffed and said, "I'll be fine, don't you worry. Just you come back and see us again sometime, okay?"

"I will," he said.

He'd never meant anything so much in all his life.

Watch for

SLOCUM AND THE RUSTLER ON THE RUN

366th novel in the exciting SLOCUM series
from Jove

Coming in August!

DON'T MISS A YEAR OF

Slocum Giant
by
Jake Logan

penguin.com/actionwesterns

M230AS0808